BECOMING THE TWILIGHT EMPRESS

FAITH L. JUSTICE

RAGGEDY MOON BOOKS

BECOMING THE TWILIGHT EMPRESS

A Theodosian Women Novella

Copyright © 2024 Faith L. Justice
All rights reserved.

2024
Raggedy Moon Books
Brooklyn, New York, USA
raggedymoonbooks.com

Cover design by Jennifer Quinlan
historicaleditorial.com

Paperback ISBN: 978-0-917053-30-6
Hardback: 978-0-917053-38-2
Epub ISBN: 978-0-917053-29-0
AudioBook ISBN: 978-0-917053-35-1
Library of Congress Control Number: 2024900295

Books by Faith L. Justice

Novels

Selene of Alexandria
Sword of the Gladiatrix (Gladiatrix #1)
Becoming the Twilight Empress (Theodosian Women #0.5)
Twilight Empress (Theodosian Women #1)
Dawn Empress (Theodosian Women #2)
Rebel Empress (Theodosian Women #3 coming in 2024)

Short Story Collections

The Reluctant Groom and Other Historical Stories
Time Again and Other Fantastic Stories
Slow Death and Other Dark Tales

Non-fiction

Hypatia, Her Life and Times

Children's Books

Tokoyo, the Samurai's Daughter (Adventurous Girls #1)

To my great friends and colleagues in the Circles in the Hair writing group.
Thirty-four years and still going strong.

"The decline of Rome was the natural and inevitable effect of immoderate greatness."

Edward Gibbon
The Decline and Fall of the Roman Empire

CONTENTS

Theodosian Genealogy

Emperors shown in SMALL CAPS.

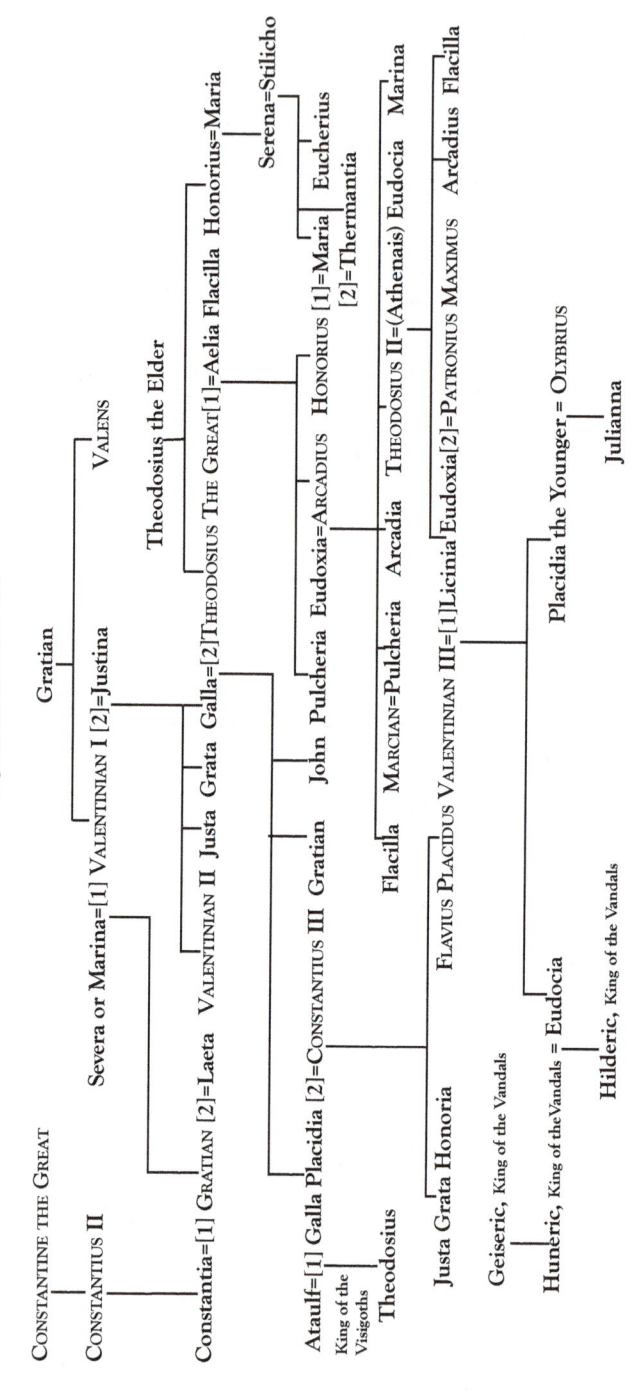

NOTE ON 5TH CENTURY ROME AND IMPERIAL TITLES

From AD 286 most Roman emperors ruled with a co-emperor; one taking the Latin-speaking western provinces and the other the Greek-speaking eastern provinces. Only a few ruled singly—among them Constantine the Great and Theodosius I. At the beginning of this story, in 408, Theodosius' younger son Honorius ruled in the West from his court in Ravenna, Italy. In Constantinople, the older son Arcadius had recently died leaving Theodosius' seven-year-old grandson Theodosius II to rule the East with the guidance of a guardian.

Imperial Roman titles evolved over time. The title AUGUSTUS (Latin for "majestic," "the increaser," or "venerable") is the equivalent of the modern "emperor," and was conferred on the first emperor, Octavian (great-nephew and adopted son of Julius Caesar), by the senate in 27 BC. Every emperor after held the title of Augustus, which always followed the family name. The first emperor conferred the title AUGUSTA on his wife, Livia, in his will. Other imperial wives (but not all) earned this supreme title. By the fifth century, sisters and daughters also could be elevated to this status, but only by a sitting Augustus. I use emperor/empress and Augustus/Augusta interchangeably throughout the text.

Octavian took his adoptive father's name, Gaius Julius Caesar, but later dropped the Gaius Julius. CAESAR became the imperial family name and was passed on by adoption. When the Julio-Claudian line died out, subsequent emperors took the name as a sign of status on their accession, adoption, or nomination as heir apparent. By the fifth century, it was the title given to any official heir to the Augustus. It's also the root of the modern titles Kaiser and Czar.

Children of imperial families were usually given the title NOBILISSIMUS/ NOBILISSIMA ("Most Noble"—boy/girl). This is the closest equivalent to the modern prince/princess, but not an exact match. The Roman title was usually conferred some years after birth, in anticipation that the child would take on higher office (Caesar or Augustus for a boy, Augusta for a girl). Throughout the text, I use the modern title princess instead of nobilissima, except on formal occasions and in correspondence.

With one exception (Constantinople for modern Istanbul), I chose to use the modern names of cities and the anglicized rather than Latin names of provinces.

CHARACTERS IN ORDER OF APPEARANCE/MENTION

(Fictional characters in italics)

Galla Placidia Noblissima—daughter of Theodosius Augustus I ("The Great") and his second wife Galla; half-sister to Flavius Honorius Augustus

Paulus—maimed Vandal soldier who served in Stilicho's household

Flavius Stilicho—Supreme army commander in the West, married to Theodosius' niece Serena, guardian during Honorius' minority as emperor, and foster father to Placidia

Serena—niece and adopted daughter of Theodosius I, wife of Stilicho, and foster mother to Placidia

Flavius Honorius Augustus—son of Theodosius I and his first wife Flacilla, Co-Emperor of Rome in the West (court located in Ravenna), and half-brother to Placidia

Alaric—General, former Roman soldier and King of the Goths

Olympius—Master of Offices under Honorius, leader of anti-barbarian faction at court

Eucherius—son of Stilicho and Serena, betrothed to Placidia

Maria Augusta—deceased older daughter of Stilicho and Serena, first wife/empress of Honorius

Thermantia Augusta (called Tia)—younger daughter of Stilicho and Serena, second wife/empress of Honorius

Flavius Constantius—General, advisor to Honorius

Heraclian—General to Honorius, later Count of Africa

Manius—Captain of Thermantia's personal guards

Marta—servants' cook in the imperial palace and Manius' love interest, Angelus' cousin

Angelus—shepherd boy and guide through Ravenna's marshes, Marta's cousin

Nepos—second in command of Thermantia's guards

Silus—one of Thermantia's guards

Gainus—Goth, former Roman soldier

Priscus Attalus—Prefect of Rome

Theonas—Senator, supporter of Attalus

Lampadius—Senator, leader of anti-barbarian faction in Rome

Laeta—second wife to Gratian Augustus (half-brother to Theodosius' second wife Galla)

Tisamene—Laeta's mother

Marion—Placidia's servant in Rome

Ataulf—General of Gothic Cavalry, former Roman soldier, and brother-in-law to King Alaric

Jovius—Master of Offices under Honorius

Flavius Theodosius Augustus II—Co-emperor of Rome in the East (court located in Constantinople), nephew of Honorius and Placidia

BECOMING THE TWILIGHT EMPRESS

PART I

THE ESCAPE

AUGUST – SEPTEMBER AD 408

CHAPTER 1

Ravenna, August 408

Placidia, Imperial Princess of the Roman Empire, skulked among the late-night shadows of Ravenna like a common thief. Her heart raced with the fear of being on her own outside of the palace—something she had never done. She wiped sweaty palms on her dark blue cloak, pulling it closer about her face. *I can do this,* she thought. *Only two more bridges and an open square.* She took a deep breath, then left the shadows for the empty streets. As she passed over the last bridge spanning a canal, she wrinkled her nose. The stench of rotting vegetation and human waste overpowered the scent of the salt sea.

The tide must be in. Perhaps Uncle Stilicho can escape by boat.

She scurried across the open plaza, crept up to a side door to the Church of St. John the Baptist, and softly knocked.

No answer.

She tried again.

No answer.

Did Uncle get my note? Am I too early? Too late? She shifted from foot to foot, trying to decide whether she should leave. Just as she turned to head home, the door opened, spilling light like liquid gold over the marble steps. A misshapen figure leaning on a crutch stood in the doorway, looking out into the dark.

"Paulus?" Placidia cried in a faint voice.

"Princess?" He squinted. "Ah, there you are," he continued, as Placidia moved closer. "Come, quickly."

1

Placidia hurried through the door. Paulus pulled it shut behind her. She found herself in a small side chapel lit with dozens of candles dripping wax onto a finely embroidered silk altar cloth. Their light threw multiple shadows, bringing flickering life to the fine mosaics of John the Baptist on the walls.

"This way." Paulus waved her to a much darker corridor. "The priests live in the other wing, and won't be about until Matins. The general is staying in the visitor's wing." He picked up a clay oil lamp in his right hand, reserving the left for his crutch. The grizzled Vandal had lost the lower part of his left leg in battle five years ago. He remarkably survived the battlefield surgeons, and had served in Stilicho's household ever since. No one was more dedicated to her uncle than Paulus.

Placidia's heart slowed as her anxiety ebbed. Soon she would see her uncle. He would make all things right.

Paulus stopped at a row of sleeping cells and rapped on the first door—three quick knocks and a pause, followed by one more knock. The door opened outward on oiled hinges, but the top hinge sagged, allowing the corner of the door to scrape the stone floor with an irritating squeal.

The light from Paulus' lamp flickered on Stilicho's face. Placidia threw herself into his arms. "Uncle, I'm so glad you're safe," she mumbled into his chest. "When Paulus sent his note, I had to come." She clung to his tall frame. Strongly built, with prematurely gray hair, Stilicho carried himself with such presence that people automatically gave way to him on the street. Even covered in mud-stained clothes and smelling of horses, he exuded an air of command. Placidia relaxed and let out a small sigh.

Stilicho bent to plant a kiss on the top of her head, hugging her tight. "My little mouse." He had called her that since becoming her guardian, because of her quiet ways and large brown eyes. Her mother died when she was five, and her emperor father the following year. Cousin Serena and her husband Stilicho took custody of her and her under-aged half-brother Emperor Honorius, adopting the familial titles of Aunt and Uncle. Stilicho released her, then looked quickly both ways down the corridor. "Let us speak more privately."

He stepped back into the cell. Placidia followed. Paulus shut the door, guarding the outside. The monk's cell was only slightly bigger than Placidia had imagined. A straw pallet on a cot took up the far wall. A folding camp chair crowded a rude wooden table, stained with ink, currently holding a pitcher of water and a flickering candle. She wrinkled her nose at the smell from the chamber pot under the bed and whispered, "Oh, Uncle."

Stilicho shrugged. "I've had worse. At least here I have a roof over my head."

"And sanctuary. Honorius can not reach you here."

"Yes, sanctuary." Her uncle looked as if he had sucked a bitter olive, then slumped onto the camp chair, lines of strain showing on his handsome face. "You should not have come, Placidia. If I had known Paulus planned to contact you, I would have stopped him."

"I am twenty and a woman grown, Uncle. I can make decisions for myself."

"But Honorius might find out and suspect you of complicity, if not treason."

"My brother may be the emperor of Rome, but he is more interested in ruling his chicken roost than his empire…at least until now." Placidia sat on the pallet by her uncle's knees and leaned her head against his shoulder. "I heard about the massacre at Pavia, but only confused reports. What happened?"

Stilicho's voice took on a weary tone. "I ordered troops to assemble there to march on the usurper in Gaul while I negotiated with the senate in Rome. I intended to pay the Goths to fight at our side. My enemies took advantage of my absence to lie to your brother, who was in Pavia to address the troops. They convinced Honorious that I intended to use the Goths to put my son on the Eastern throne and take the Western throne for myself." He shook his head. "The young fool! Honorius believed them. My enemies orchestrated a riot. The army murdered every high-ranking official in attendance."

"Blessed Mother of God." Blood drained from Placidia's face. "All?"

"All who owed their positions to me." Stilicho rubbed his face and pushed back a lock of greasy hair. His eyes unfocussed as if picturing the men in his mind. "Generals, provincial prefects, the treasurer, and so many more. Good men…true to the empire. I came to Ravenna to secure the garrison against further riot but found Honorius had ordered my arrest." Stilicho slumped forward, head in hands.

"Why would my brother do such a thing?" she cried. "You've kept his empire safe during his minority, showing your loyalty time and again by protecting our borders. What stirred our normally placid Honorius to such drastic action?"

"Not what, but who. That snake Olympius, leader of the anti-barbarian faction, has been much in your brother's company this summer, and we know that whoever has the emperor's ear has his will." Stilicho sighed. "Serena warned me I should keep Honorius with me on the battlefield, but I didn't want to risk his life."

Placidia chewed at her lower lip in concentration. "Surely, Uncle, we can recover my brother's affection for you. After all, we have double ties of blood—his marriage to your daughter and my betrothal to your son. My half-witted brother must at least acknowledge your loyalty. No one has worked harder than you to bring about peace in our empire."

"There are many at court who are not my friends." Stilicho scratched at his short beard. "After all these years, they are jealous of my power, and they cannot forget my father was a Vandal. It galls proud Romans to believe their honor and safety lies in the hands of the son of a barbarian, even though I've known no other life than that of a Roman. The more honors I earn, the deeper their hatred runs. Now their faction has the upper hand."

"I can convince my brother of your loyalty." Placidia took her uncle's calloused hands in her soft ones. "I will go to him tomorrow. Then you can leave this wretched place."

"Many is the time I've regretted that Roman law does not allow females to rule in their own name, Placidia, for you are the only one of Theodosius' children to take after him. It is my eternal frustration that I could not raise your brothers to be the leaders this empire needs in these troubled times." Stilicho shook his head. "But it is too late for me. My enemies have won. I and my son are traitors in your brother's mind."

"Treason?" Fear widened Placidia's eyes. Her breath caught in her throat. "Where is Eucherius?" Stilicho's son held no title or position of power and seemed to have no ambition other than to write poetry. Placidia loved her betrothed with the tender protectiveness of a friend or older sister.

"Some of my men are taking him to Serena in Rome."

"He will be safe with his mother." Even as she said it, Placidia knew that wasn't necessarily true. Treason was a stench that clung to a person even when falsely accused. "You must stay here in sanctuary until I can persuade my brother to meet with you and give you fair trial. Honorius is many things, but even the emperor would not break the law of sanctuary."

"My brave little mouse." Stilicho pulled Placidia into a tight hug. "We must make plans to save you and Tia in case of failure. I have good men in the palace, loyal to my family. I'll get word to them."

4

"Tia?" Placida buried a small twinge of guilt. She hadn't told her cousin about meeting Stilicho, out of concern for her health. "Surely Honorius would not hurt his own wife? She is your daughter, but frail, and no threat to him."

"Our history is filled with assassinated empresses. If my enemies want to eliminate my family, they will do it with or without the emperor's consent."

"Then I cannot fail." Deadly fear for her adoptive family constricted Placidia's chest. "I must convince Honorius to reconcile with you."

He tipped up her chin and asked, "What's the first rule of battle?"

"A good general always has a way to retreat, so as to fight again."

"Be a good general. Now go, before someone discovers you are missing. You don't want Honorius to doubt your loyalty." Stilicho knocked on the door. Paulus opened it.

Placidia turned to her uncle one last time. "God bless and keep you safe." *And God give me the strength to protect the ones I love.*

CHAPTER 2

The next morning, Thermantia, Empress of the Western Roman Empire, sobbed in Placidia's arms. "Father is accused of treason and Honorius says he will repudiate me, because we never consummated the marriage. As if that's my fault!"

Placidia patted her cousin's back. "Oh, Tia!" She felt slightly muddled from lack of sleep, but fear—and Tia's distress—sharpened her focus. *What is Honorius up to? Are Uncle's enemies moving so quickly against innocent Tia? All the more reason I must not fail at my meeting with my brother.*

She hugged Tia closer. Her cousin was frail at twenty-two; unnaturally pale, constantly tired, and plagued with a persistent cough. The same symptoms of the disease that had carried off her older sister Maria, the previous empress, a year earlier. Placidia unconsciously strengthened her hold.

"Honorius was a nasty boy, and he grew into a nastier man," Tia spat. Gaining spirit with her anger, she pulled out of Placidia's arms. "He has more interest in his pet chickens than he ever did in me. Why did my father force me to marry such a monster?"

"He's not a monster, Tia, just—" Placidia groped for the right word. "—unfinished. Caught somewhere between child and man." She suspected her older half-brother suffered from an affliction. Although twenty-four, he had yet to exhibit all the physical signs of an adult male. He sported a scant brown beard, his body soft and temperament lethargic. Most damning of all—according to his wife—he lacked the ability to procreate. Placidia blushed at the thought.

Familiar with breeding horses and dogs, she had a working knowledge of the physical sex act and was shocked when Tia had told her she was still a virgin after a year of marriage.

Placidia clasped one of her cousin's pale, cold hands and sighed. "Wasn't it better to stay here with your family than be married off to some Persian prince or ancient senator? I'm sure your father thought not only to bind our families closer, but to protect you, as well." Placidia was grateful her own engagement to Eucherius forestalled such an unwanted fate.

"I'm sorry I spoke so hastily. I know the marriage was for the best." Tia wiped the tears from her face and blew her nose on a linen kerchief. "Here I am, crying over possibly being put aside, when I prayed to be free this whole past year. Free of Honorius and free of those dreadful court duties."

"And free of all those simpering ladies looking for advantage for their husbands and sons." Placidia smiled, knowing how the traditional crowd of senator's wives and other noble ladies assigned to the empress irritated her cousin. "I haven't seen a one since Honorius arrived at the palace."

Tia almost smiled; then fresh tears brimmed in her eyes. "But, Father! What am I to do?"

"I know, Sweeting." Placidia smoothed her cousin's hair. "It's a tangled skein, but I have good news! Your father is in Ravenna. He claimed sanctuary at the Church of St. John. I met with him last night—"

"You met with him? Father's here?" Tia's eyes grew round. "You left the palace on your own? How is he? Where's Eucherius? What are his plans?"

"One question at a time, Cousin!" Placidia laughed. "He's fine. We have a plan." She recounted her adventures and conversations of the past evening. "I'm to meet with Honorius later today and plead your father's case."

Tia grabbed her hand. Her voice shook. "Be careful with him, Placidia. Honorius is afraid, and lashing out. I have little sympathy for your brother, but what happened at Pavia terrified him. He told me the soldiers killed a man at his feet as he begged Honorius for mercy. He sees conspirators everywhere! Even imperial sisters can be accused of treason."

Placidia's blood chilled. *How can I do this? What if I fail?*

THAT AFTERNOON, Placidia dressed with care for her audience with her brother. Her servants helped her into a shimmering pink stola embroidered with green vines around the neck, hem, and sleeves; layered over a virginal white linen tunica. The colors flattered her rosy skin and dark hair.

"This, my Lady?" A servant held up a gold girdle designed to emphasize her small breasts.

"No." Placidia shook her head. "I think that one." She pointed to a low-slung gold link belt.

Her hairdresser arranged her dark tresses in a simple chignon at the back of her neck—as befitted a young unmarried woman—with a row of curls framing her face. As a finishing touch, she donned the emerald necklace and earrings Honorius had given her two years ago, for her eighteenth birthday, along with four gold bracelets from her mother.

"You look lovely!" her servant gushed. Placidia looked in the mirror and took the compliment with skepticism. She had the advantage of healthy youth but knew she wasn't classically beautiful. Her nose was too long and mouth too wide. And she was too thin! Men seemed to favor girls with more flesh on their bones. She smiled at her conceit. She wasn't planning to seduce her brother, but to persuade him to a more rational course.

Having finished her toilet, she proceeded to her audience, trailed by her ever-present guards. Her silk slippers whispered on the marble floors. The creaking of leather armor echoed off frescoed walls. Servants and courtiers retreated to the sides of the corridors, bowing their heads as she passed.

She liked the palace in Ravenna. It was a large mansion—not near as fine as the collection of imperial palaces which inhabited the entire Palatine Hill in Rome, but homier, much easier to navigate. Her father, the Great Theodosius Augustus, had moved the court from Rome to Milan to be closer to the border and the armies he led against barbarians and usurpers. After his death, Honorius moved the court to Ravenna to cower behind impenetrable swamps. Other men—like Stilicho—led his armies. The thought of her uncle in sanctuary stiffened Placidia's resolve.

Before she reached the audience chamber, a skinny page stopped to bow before her. "Most Gracious Princess, I bring a message from Our Most Esteemed Emperor."

"Speak." She tapped her foot, trying to tamp down her impatience. *Is Honorius trying to avoid me?*

"Our Gracious Augustus asked me to lead you to his…uh…personal…uh…"

"If he wants to meet me in his suite, say so, boy."

"No, Princess. Please follow me." He looked at her with such dismay, she had to suppress a smile.

Placidia and her guard followed the page through unfamiliar back corridors to a dusty sun-drenched garden which revealed the reason for the boy's concern. Honorius chose to meet her in his chicken yard. The page started sneezing within moments of entering the enclosure.

"Please, your Hidness…?" The poor boy's eyes teared; his nose ran. "Achoo!" He pulled a ragged kerchief from his sleeve, trying to stem the flow.

A reaction to the dust? The chickens?

"You're excused, boy." She told him softly, handing him a clean kerchief. "Go see the physician."

"Tank youd." The page bobbed his head and retreated with a grateful smile.

"Welcome, Princess Placidia. We see too little of you at court."

The familiar voice sent an unwelcome shiver up her spine. She turned.

General Constantius greeted her. On first meeting Constantius, she had taken an instant dislike to the man. Others thought him genial and honest, and he had fought with distinction under her father and uncle. But, physically, he was the opposite of Stilicho—dark complexion, an absurdly long neck, topped by a broad head. His bulbous eyes shifted from side to side, rarely meeting hers. Most condemning of all, he was awkward on a horse. He leaned low over the animal's neck and always looked about to fall off. Placidia was a superb rider, having been taught by Stilicho himself. It might be unfair to judge a man on his appearance and riding skills, but, as her brother's friend and confidant, Constantius was suspect.

"I only recently set up my own household, General. Managing it takes much of my time," Placidia said coldly. A wounded look flashed so quickly across Constantius' face, she wondered if she imagined it. She set aside the puzzle of the general for another day. She had a mission, and she mustn't fail. She spied Honorius in a corner, holding a particularly large rooster with glossy black feathers.

He waved to her. "Placidia, come see."

She immediately regretted her finery—particularly her dainty silk slippers— while negotiating chicken droppings. As she approached, the rooster flapped its wings, stirring the dusty air and crying raucously. Constantius followed her across the courtyard but hovered awkwardly, two paces away, as she approached her brother.

"Isn't he magnificent?" Honorius held the rooster aloft and chuckled. "I call him Rome because he is so great and noisy!"

"Brother, I had hoped we might speak in private." Placidia coughed and waved to one of the ubiquitous servants for a cup of water. She sipped the chilled lemon-infused drink, soothing her throat.

"Constantius is my dearest friend." Honorius nodded at the general. "He will soon be off to put down that usurper from Britain. What you say to me can be heard by him. Besides, I have a proposal for you, my dear." He put the rooster down and turned to her with a satisfied grin.

Her stomach flopped at the thought of what her brother might have in store for her. Placidia put on a pleasant but serious face. "I've come to speak to you of our Uncle Stilicho."

"He's no uncle of mine or yours, just our cousin's husband," Honorius spat. "He's a traitor. Anyone who defends him is a traitor as well."

"Our wise and honored father made him guardian of both of us—"

Honorius interrupted. "We have only Stilicho's word for that. Father left no written instructions."

"Bishop Ambrose was also at Father's deathbed, and he vouches for Stilicho." Placidia took her brother's arm and walked him away from Constantius. "Besides, you were but ten years old. Who else could hold the empire for you but Father's most trusted general, and husband to his beloved niece? For fourteen years Stilicho has served us well. What quarrel do you have with him?"

"I'm of age to rule on my own and have been for years!" He puffed out his chest, like one of his roosters. "But Stilicho treats me like a child!"

"You rule the empire, Brother, no other. Your name must be on all laws and declarations to be valid." She tried to soothe his wounded pride. "But unless you want to lead the armies yourself, you need good generals."

"Constantius is a good general and loyal to me."

"As is Stilicho."

"He seeks my death!" Honorius' voice wavered; his body shivered. His eyes shot from place to place, as if searching for hidden assassins.

"No, Honorius." She turned to face him, taking both his hands in hers. Her heart raced; blood flushed her cheeks as she realized how deeply Honorius feared for his life. Tia was right. Pavia had deeply affected her brother. She strove to keep the desperation from her voice. "Stilicho seeks only to serve you and Rome. He seeks only your glory."

"Then why does he conspire with that rebellious barbarian General Alaric to overthrow me and give my empire to the Goths?"

"He does no such thing! What proofs have you?" Placidia felt her confidence slipping. Usually Honorius would listen to her, but today he was mulish. Not a good sign.

"He could have destroyed Alaric several times over, yet always let him get away. He demands the Roman Senate pay that so-called king four thousand pounds in gold and award the extortionist the title of *magister militum* of Illyricum. Master of the Militia! That's an outrage to the honor of Rome."

"Four thousand pounds of gold is not much. It is little more than the annual income of a senator, and not the richest senator at that!" She chuckled, trying to lighten his mood. "Is not a bit of gold and a title worth the price of peace on our borders in these perilous times? With General Alaric and his Gothic warriors protecting the eastern provinces from the Huns, you can concentrate on destroying this usurper who invaded Gaul."

Honorius gripped her hands and squeezed as he hissed at her. "I have it on good authority that Stilicho plans to install his son as co-emperor. Is it not bad enough he forced his two sickly daughters on me in marriage? I have to share my diadem with Eucherius?" He released her, throwing her hands away in disgust.

This change in her brother's attitude was much worse than she thought. Placidia recognized another man's arguments in her brother's rants. Tia's warning echoed in her mind; *even imperial sisters can be accused of treason. Am I in danger?*

She tried to soothe him with a touch on his arm. "I lived in Stilicho's household for over ten years, Brother. I would know if anything threatened you and would be by your side immediately."

"Would you?" Honorius gave her a bone-chilling grin. "My always loyal *half-sister?* How long will I live, once you and Eucherius are married and have a child?" He mimed wringing a chicken's neck. "My life won't be worth a lead coin."

"Honorius, we're family!" She stepped closer. "Don't listen to the envious words of strangers. They are greedy for position and power."

"And you are not?" Honorius put his hand on her breast, fondling it.

"Brother, you go too far!" Placidia gasped and backed away, blood flooding her face. Her eyes sought Constantius, hovering several feet away. Would he help? He lurched forward; his face contorted with... fear? Rage? He froze, then turned his head away. She lifted her chin. *Cowardly sycophant!*

11

Her brother pouted. "See! You will not even allow me to show you affection. How can I trust you to look out for my interests?"

"I do look out for your interests." Blood pounded in her ears. She wanted to slap Honorius silly, but forced herself to breathe deeply and continue with her petition. "There is no proof of Stilicho's treason, just the tales of jealous courtiers. By settling General Alaric and his people on our border, as our father intended, you make them into allies. You give them a home to defend against the Huns."

"I don't trust the barbarians. There are too many of them in positions of power—in the court and in the army. They will turn on me."

"Not Stilicho, and not Eucherius." Placidia controlled the urge to tap her foot. "They do not seek the diadem. They seek only to serve you."

"I will thwart their clever plans," Honorius continued, as if she hadn't spoken. "General Constantius has proposed marriage to you. I'm considering it. He's a loyal friend and it would take you away from Stilicho's influence."

Placidia's heart sank at the depth of suspicion poisoning her brother's soul. Nothing she said seemed to deter him. She might save herself through marriage, but the thought of Constantius as her husband brought bile to her throat. She bowed slightly in the general's direction and prayed to God for forgiveness for a lie. "I'm honored by the proposal, but I'm considering a life in Christ."

"A pledged virgin!" Honorius laughed and sidled closer, almost whispering in her ear. "Since when, Placidia? You've taken no vows." Her skin crawled as he confronted her, both hands gripping her wrists. "I know this is a popular way for women to avoid marriage but, as your brother and emperor, I command you. You cannot take vows or marry without my permission. You will do as I say!" His voice ended in a near shout as he flung down her wrists and stomped to the table that held chilled wine and silver goblets. The chickens clucked in panic, avoiding his feet. A quaking servant poured him a large drink.

Placidia rubbed her arms where bruises would spot her flesh on the morrow. She remembered her uncle's advice, plan for retreat, to fight another day. She bowed her head in seeming submission. "Honorius, I will do as you say. I only ask that you take some consideration of my wishes when you make your decision about my marriage. I am your loving sister, not a horse to be bartered away for prestige or property."

"I know perfectly well your value, and I've made no decisions—yet." He waved to his companion. "Constantius, come join us. Your suit is favorable in my eyes, but, as my sister reminded me, she is a valuable commodity. I cannot give her to just anyone."

Placidia had no desire to continue her fruitless petition or remain in her brother's company. The bitter taste of failure lingered in her throat, like the aftertaste of vomit. She wanted only to escape and plan her next moves. "May I be excused, Brother? It is hot, and the smell of the birds makes my stomach weak."

"Of course." Honorius waved his hand as if shooing a fly from a piece of fruit.

Placidia fled.

CHAPTER 3

After recovering her composure and changing out of her finery, Placidia sought her cousin, to tell her the troubling news. She found her in the palace solar, a pleasant place filled with the scent of late summer roses blooming in pots and the tinkling sound of water falling from a central fountain. Tia sat on padded bench; an open book abandoned in her lap.

A Gospel? Or poetry?

Placidia waved at the trio of servants standing by with food and drink, "You may go." She sat quietly next to Tia until the servants left.

"I can tell from your face that your talk with my husband didn't go well." Tia frowned.

"No. He is convinced his life is in danger from the barbarians and that your father conspires with them. He believes my marriage to Eucherius is part of the conspiracy and proposes I marry General Constantius…" Placidia's voice trailed off as she dropped her head into her hands. "I don't know what to do. He won't listen to reason."

This time it was Tia who consoled Placidia, with a comforting arm around her shoulders.

"I knew my brother was shaken by Pavia, but I had no idea how it disturbed his mind." Placidia sat up. "Are you in danger, Tia?"

"I hope not—now." A small secretive smile crossed her face as she leaned in to whisper, "The captain of my household guards came to me. He had received word from my father and pledged his loyalty to me again. I sent him to meet with Father and see what plans he had for us."

"Good. Stilicho will know what to do." A small glimmer of hope flamed in Placidia. *Yes, I failed, but Uncle will save us. We can all escape…*

"Mistress, forgive me." A female servant entered the room. "Captain Manius awaits your pleasure. He says it is urgent."

"Yes! Send him in at once!" Tia squeezed Placidia's hand.

A young man, with the broad shoulders and well-muscled limbs of a professional soldier, strode past the servant, growling, "Leave us!"

To her credit, the girl glanced at Tia for permission before abandoning her post.

The captain looked pale and agitated. He came to attention before Tia and said, in a deep voice, "I bring terrible news, Augusta. General Stilicho is dead."

Shock froze Placidia. *Uncle can't be dead. He's safe in sanctuary. He will save us, take us away from this nightmare!*

"Augusta!" Manius rushed forward as her cousin slumped, whimpering in pain. Placidia caught her before she fell to the floor. Tia's eyes rolled up, showing only the whites. Her face froze in a rictus of horror.

"Tia! Tia!" Placidia shook her cousin.

Manius wrapped Tia in his cloak. "Forgive my familiarity, Princess. The Augusta is in a nervous state. She needs warmth and liquids. I've seen this before, in wounded men."

"Of course. We should get her to her quarters, put her to bed, and call a physician."

The captain lifted her cousin as if she were a small child and carried her out of the room. Placidia shouted orders to the servants as they passed.

They settled Tia in her warmed bed under the care of her physician and a flock of servants. Placidia sighed. Her immediate worry about her cousin subsided, leaving her shaky. "Doctor, I'll be right outside. Call me when she wakes, or anything changes."

Placidia looked at the warm bed with envy but pulled herself together. "Captain, I wish to know more. Join me."

"Of course, Princess."

They settled on cushioned chairs in the anteroom decorated with soothing greens, pinks, and grays—geometric marble on the floors and a garden scene frescoed on the walls. Niches in the walls held pots of cut flowers; a small censor wafted sandalwood scent. Placidia dismissed the servants after accepting a silver goblet of rich red wine.

She gave the captain a couple moments to gratefully gulp from his cup while she sipped. The need for action wore off; deadly lethargy threatened to overwhelm her. She wanted only to go to her own bed and deny this day ever happened, but needed to know more if she were to help her cousin and herself.

"Captain. Were you present at my uncle's death, or did you hear the news second hand?"

"I saw the dastardly assassination."

"I thought Uncle was in sanctuary."

"He was tricked into leaving."

Placidia grew impatient with the man's short answers. "Captain, I am not a delicate flower. I wish to know what you know."

"It is not a pretty tale, Princess." The captain's face creased with concern, his dark eyes hooded and wary.

"I do not blame the messenger. Please, tell me the whole story."

"The Augusta sent me to meet with General Stilicho at the Church of St. John. I had just entered the nave with a small escort when a delegation from the emperor arrived demanding to speak to Stilicho, as well."

"Who were in the delegation?"

"General Heraclian, Master of Offices Olympius, and a unit of imperial guards."

"Master of Offices Olympius? Since when?" Placidia asked in alarm. Master of Offices was a powerful post, controlling the civil service and, more importantly, the messenger and intelligence gathering corps known as *agentes in rebus*. He also dictated court ceremonies, supervised the imperial guard, and controlled access to the emperor—critical functions if one wanted to control the emperor himself. It looked like Olympius now ruled the emperor who ruled Rome. She chewed her lower lip until the captain gave a soft grunt. She looked up as he raised an eyebrow.

"Continue, Captain."

"Olympius came into the church while the others waited outside in the plaza. He conferred with the bishop and Stilicho, claiming he was only there to arrest the general for later trial. I begged your uncle not to leave sanctuary, but he believed the message to be from Honorius. He said, 'I am innocent of this charge. I raised Honorius to be a good and fair man. He will restore me to my place.' When General Stilicho passed the holy threshold and reached the plaza, the guards arrested him. I watched as…" Manius paused to take a deep drink

16

of wine. "I watched as General Heraclian produced an order of execution from your brother naming Stilicho a traitor and regicide."

"You did nothing to help?" Placidia accused.

Manius flinched. "I tried." He looked Placidia straight in the eyes. "I ordered my men to follow me to rescue the general. We stormed out of the church; swords drawn. Everyone would gladly have died for Stilicho, but he stopped us. We were badly outnumbered." Tears glittered in the captain's eyes. "He told us to stand down, declaring, 'I have always obeyed my emperor, and will do so even in this.' He bowed his head. Heraclian took it off with his sword. Your uncle was a brave and honorable man."

"Oh!" Placidia gasped. Pain knifed through her stomach to her heart. She clasped herself tightly with both arms, trying to hold the tears inside. Looking up at the worried Manius, she took a deep breath. "What of you and your men, Captain? Are you in danger for trying to save my uncle?"

"I don't think Olympius is after such small fish as us, but I do worry about the Augusta." He glanced at the closed door. "Do you know if the rumors are true? Will the emperor cast her off?"

"Yes. He has told her so."

"Please tell her that I and my men are at her service for whatever she needs. I swore an oath to her father when he assigned me to guard her, and renewed that vow to her today. I will honor that oath even unto my death."

"Let us hope that is not necessary, Captain." She rose, holding out a hand. "I will confer with my cousin. I fear for her, as well. We may need to move quickly. Thank you for your pledge of loyalty."

He rose and took her hand, kissing the signet ring on her index finger. "Thank you, Princess. Please do not delay in your plans. Events are moving swiftly. So should you."

"Out! All of you!" Placidia dismissed her people. Body servants, dressers, hair and make-up slaves, chamber maids, all scurried from her pain and anger.

Alone. A rare state for an imperial princess, and the second time in two days she had demanded it. *Much good it did Uncle that I escaped the palace. I failed, and he's dead!*

Placidia curled up on her bed, clutched a silk cushion, and moaned, letting loose the grief she couldn't show in front of her cousin, Manius, or the servants. Her breath came in ragged bursts, punctuated by chest-tearing sobs.

Uncle Stilicho is dead.

She had experienced her parents' deaths as a child. Their loss, an absence of distant figures, a vague anxiety as to who would take care of her. Her nurse cared for her day-to-day, providing the love and nurture she needed. When Serena and Stilicho took charge of her and Honorius, they welcomed the children to their own household, gave them the gift of lively cousins. Placidia smiled at memories of romps in the nursery as the mighty general stooped to let the children ride "horsey."

Her oldest cousin, Maria, and Honorius turned up their noses at such childish pursuits; but Tia, Eucherius, and Placidia squealed with delight as Stilicho galloped around the room, snorting and rearing. As she grew older, there were real horses, as well as family discussions of Homer and Virgil, and—most important—information about the state of the empire her brother would rule.

Uncle never imagined this world! The mighty Roman Empire beset as never before, with a weak-minded emperor and enemies both within and without. Without Stilicho's strong hand at the helm, who will hold the empire together? Who will order my life—a young woman, unwed, a pawn in imperial politics? Olympius? Constantius? Honorius?

Placidia shuddered. *No good answers there.*

The storm of her grief passed, and the pain receded to a throbbing ache. Her uncle was dead, but her Aunt Serena lived in Rome and her cousin Eucherius hid there from his enemies. *Uncle is not here. I must get Tia to Rome and the safety of Aunt Serena.*

"Be a good general," she echoed her uncle's words. Placidia wiped the tears from her cheeks and sat up. *I have planning to do.*

CHAPTER 4

Imperial Palace and the marshes surrounding Ravenna, August 408

I t's time," Placidia gently shook her cousin's shoulder. "Let's go home to Rome; to your mother."

"So soon?" Tia rolled over in her bed, knuckling her eyes and yawning. She sat up, her feet automatically searching for her sandals. Lamplight flickered on her face, emphasizing the lines of grief etched there. Placidia surmised her own face mirrored her cousin's.

Within days of Stilicho's death, Olympius had arrested anyone even remotely connected with Stilicho and questioned them concerning the so-called conspiracy. Even under torture, no evidence of Stilicho's guilt came to light. Neither Placidia nor Tia had heard from Eucherius. They prayed he had reached Rome safely.

When Honorius formally divorced his empress, she extracted his promise that she could "retire" safely to her mother's home in Rome. Tia made hasty plans to leave Ravenna before Honorius changed his mind or Olympius could convince him to revoke her pardon.

Placidia planned to leave with her cousin. She didn't ask Honorius' permission. She knew the answer.

"Stay here in Ravenna with your brother," Tia had argued. "You need to separate yourself from our family in his eyes."

"If I stay, I fear Honorius will force me to marry General Constantius." Placidia shuddered, recalling Constantius' covetous gaze when she last attended court. "Besides, I don't trust Olympius. I've heard rumors you will be in danger on the road. It would suit him if fake bandits or, better yet, rogue barbarians attacked and killed you. He would be rid of another of Stilicho's children and have more evidence of the evil barbarians with which to rouse fear."

"Then don't put yourself in danger."

Placida tightened her jaw and raised her chin. "I would rather hazard my life with you on the road to Rome than stay here and be the subject of my brother's whims."

Tia had nodded. Either path held its dangers.

Now the time had come.

Tia looked around her sumptuous room, showing no regret, until she spied a rudely carved wooden doll abandoned on the floor next to an empty trunk. She walked over and picked it up. Her face crumpled. "My father—" Her voice caught. "—made this for me." Tia slumped to the floor, then sobbed. "The empire can go to hell."

Placidia sat next to her. "You don't mean that, Cousin."

Tia scrubbed her face with her hands. "No, I don't. I love the empire and all it stands for—peace, grace, learning—civilization in all its glory, but I hate what it's done to my family."

"I know. It grieves me that my gullible brother and evil petty men can wound you so." Placidia looked at the backs of her hands, then turned them over to stare at the soft palms. She clenched them into tight fists. "If I had only been able to persuade my brother from his course, your father would be alive."

"You did what you could, Placidia. I was his wife, and could not influence him. Put the blame where it belongs—on that piece of horseshit, Olympius."

Placidia, taken aback at her gentle cousin's mild profanity, smiled. "I think that defames horseshit."

Tia returned the smile, dried her tears, and rose from the floor. "Come. Let us go to Rome."

Her cousin dressed in a linen tunica, warm wool stola the color of dried blood, and a dark blue cloak—all devoid of the gold embroidery and glittering jewels typical of court wear. Placidia already wore similar serviceable travel clothes—warm for August, but they would travel over mountains. Both carried only a few personal items from their toilet, small sacks of travel money, and their favorite jewels. Servants had packed the few possessions Tia cared to take, in two hampers. She added the wooden doll.

Placidia supported Tia down the hall to the atrium. There, men dressed in anonymous livery loaded supplies on their broad shoulders and disappeared through the doorway towards the back of the palace. Placidia motioned to Manius. "Captain, we're ready."

Tia looked around. "Where is that silly servant? I told her to meet us here."

"I dismissed her," Placidia replied. "It is better if I serve you on the road. People seldom notice servants, so I can travel anonymously."

"What a clever idea!" Tia suppressed a coughing fit and leaned heavily against Placidia's shoulder.

Placidia gave the captain a worried look. He nodded.

"Forgive me." Manius picked Tia up, producing a small gasp from the frail woman. "The landing's this way, Augusta." He thrust his chin in the direction of the doorway.

"I'm no longer an augusta, Captain. Address me as Mistress."

"You will always be Augusta to us...Mistress."

Placidia followed through the corridors, her heart racing at the possibility of being discovered. *What would Honorius do if he caught me leaving the court without his permission? Prison? Death? Marriage?* She shivered at the thought. *Of the last two, which was worse?*

After a few moments in the servant corridors, they exited to a boat landing normally used to deliver supplies. Placidia blinked, adjusting her eyes to the pre-dawn gloom. Canals, filled with water from the Po River and flushed regularly by the Adriatic tides, crisscrossed Ravenna. Everyone in the small city traveled by boat, barge, or bridge. Nearly impassable marshes bounded the landside.

The captain settled Tia in the bow of a boat and turned to offer a calloused hand to Placidia. The sturdy square-bottomed craft swayed gently under her weight as she made her way to the front and sat beside her cousin. A warm mist swirled about them. The stench of stagnant water filled with refuse rose with it. Tia began to cough—deep, retching sounds that echoed over the water.

The captain looked back at the palace in alarm, should the sound bring palace guards down on them.

Placidia thumped her cousin's back.

"My bag," Tia gasped. "Medicine." Placidia searched her cousin's bag and discovered a stoppered vial. She handed the jar to Tia, who took a swallow. The potion smelled of cherries and wine. Placidia recognized another, more bitter scent. *Ah, poppy juice!*

A few more deep coughs, and they tapered off. Tia shivered. Placidia put her arms about her cousin. The exhausted woman promptly fell asleep, her head on Placidia's shoulder. *I didn't expect the poppy juice to work so fast. Perhaps it's for the best.*

The guards loaded more bundles into the boat, then boarded. More men and bundles occupied a second boat. One of the guards pushed off from the wharf with a pole; two others on each side took up oars. Synchronizing their movements, they rowed the vessel into the middle of the channel, followed quietly by the second boat.

The eastern sky lightened. Soon, the canals would teem with craft bringing goods to the markets. The red dawn tinged the buildings with color. Placidia shivered at the ill omen—*blood, or fire?*

They continued through the by-ways and shortly came to the marshes. They rowed up an inlet and onto a muddy bank. A ragamuffin boy stood under a dying tree in a water meadow, chatting with a man guarding a covered wagon and a small herd of horses. The captain again lifted Tia in his arms and carried her ashore. She turned sleepily, curling into his shoulder, murmuring what sounded to Placidia's ears like, "Papa, is that you?"

Even in the dim dawn light, Placidia saw the blood rush to the captain's face. "Pay her no mind. It's the medicine." She lifted a hand to her cousin's cheek. "No sign of fever, thank God."

Manius nodded; relief lightened his face. "I'll settle her in the wagon, Princess."

She turned at the scrape of the second boat pulling onto the bank. Another contingent of guards came ashore with supplies. Placidia moved out of their way, toward the wagon. The raggedy boy approached Manius hesitantly. Was the child afraid of the soldier? In the increasing light, she got a better look at him. Ten, maybe twelve? His dark curly hair needed cutting, and the dirt ground into his bare knees and around his fingernails looked permanent. *What is his role in this journey?*

The boy cleared his throat.

"What do you want, boy?" Manius asked, irritated, continuing to direct the other men. "I'm busy."

"The wagon, Sir."

"What about it?" The captain turned his full glare on the boy.

"I don't think it will get through the marsh. It's too heavy and too tall."

Is this child our guide through the swamp? Such a slim reed on which to balance our safety! Placidia began to have doubts about the captain's plan.

"You told me you could get a wagon through." Manius crossed his arms over his chest, frowning.

"You said a cart. I thought it would be much smaller. The bed is too wide. That tent on the wagon will show above the grass when we near the road to Rome, as will mounted horses. You should pack what you can on the horses and mules and go on foot. That's much safer and faster. We can take a more direct route on narrower paths if we go on foot, single file."

Manius' face turned red as a flaring coal, then paled. He shook his head and uncrossed his arms. "The Augusta is ill and must ride in a covered wagon."

"The only path that will take that monster will cross the main road. I thought the whole point of going through the swamps was to avoid patrols."

"It is." The captain glanced at the wagon. "We'll have to cross at night."

A dark frown marred the boy's face as he retreated toward the horses, muttering under his breath.

"So that's our guide?" Placidia arched an eyebrow at Manius.

"The boy comes highly recommended by my...uh...by the servants' cook, Marta. He's her cousin." The soldier blushed under his deep tan. "I didn't want to trust a huntsman from the palace."

"I understand." Placidia offered a small smile. *It looks like our captain is more than friendly with this Marta or he wouldn't trust her judgement where Tia's life is concerned.* She wandered past the boy to check the horses. Looking them over, she picked the best of the herd—a black gelding with three white socks—and stroked its neck, murmuring. The warm animal smell of the horse brought unwanted memories of Stilicho. She swallowed a sob, then turned to inspect the peasant boy standing nearby.

He met her gaze with a bold look.

Indicating her modest clothes, he smiled impudently. "Manius called you 'Princess.' You don't look like no princess I've ever seen."

Placidia grinned at the boy. "Have you seen many?"

"I've seen plenty." He puffed out his meager chest. "I've been to the palace!"

Placidia sniffed and held her nose. "To deliver fish?"

The boy laughed, his voice echoing over the water. "I catch tasty fish."

"What else do you do?"

"I tend my gran's sheep and I know all the best places to snare ducks. No one knows the marshes like Angelus." He thumped his chest. "I'm to be your guide past the patrols."

"Angelus?" Placidia chuckled over such an incongruous name for the impish lad.

The boy looked as if he'd sucked a sour lemon. He scuffed his feet in the dirt. "That was my gran's idea. My mom died birthin' me. I nearly died too. Gran fed me sheep's milk and called me her 'little angel' as she had no one else to care for."

"Well, you'll be my little angel today." She wagged a finger at him. "If you get us safely past the patrols."

Manius finished ordering their escort and joined them. "Is the boy bothering you, Prin—"

Placidia shook her head.

A cunning look crossed the boy's face.

"Not at all, Captain. He was just explaining his prowess at fishing, herding, and evading capture."

Manius frowned, rubbing his jaw. "Marta says he's a good lad, Lady, but prone to exaggeration. Don't put too much store in what he says."

The cunning look gave way to one of stormy indignation. "I'm the best at these marshes. See how far you get without me." Angelus turned to stomp off.

Manius grabbed the boy's tunic by the back of the neck. "Hold it, son. I never said you couldn't get us through the marshes. I'm counting on it. I just don't want you bothering the lady with your tall tales."

"I'll not be bothering the 'lady'." Angelus bowed to Manius and tugged at his forelock. "Unless she asks," he muttered out of the side of his mouth.

Manius gave the boy a sharp look, then took Placidia by the elbow. "It's time we moved on. My mistress awaits inside." He indicated the mule-drawn wagon.

Built on the barbarian model, the wagon had room for two sleeping pallets as well as bundles of supplies. An ingenious covered frame provided shelter over the wagon bed. Eyeing the heavy vehicle, Placidia had her own misgivings about getting it through the marshes. Tia slept on a pallet amid bundles of clothes and baskets of food. *Perhaps she could be carried on a litter?* Placidia glanced at the dawn sky darkening with clouds. *No, Manius was right. Tia needed to be sheltered.*

The idea of sitting in the back, jolting with every step, made Placidia's stomach queasy. She walked to the front and asked, "Driver, do you mind if I join you?"

"You can keep me company anytime, Princess." The driver turned his grizzled head.

"Paulus! I thought Olympius and his thrice-cursed followers captured you along with my uncle." Joy coursed through her at the sight of the old soldier. She hitched up her skirts, climbed the wagon wheel, and scrambled onto the seat to give Paulus a hug.

"My master bade me stay in sanctuary. I had to watch that shameful murder from the door of the church." The old warrior clenched his teeth. "But they didn't want the likes of me. I've been hiding and keeping in touch with Manius, waiting for some opportunity to be of service to your family."

"Thank you. Few are so loyal." She wiped a tear from her cheek. Paulus ducked his head. Placidia ignored his strangled sob. After giving him a moment to recover, she asked, "How's the leg today?" Paulus had astonished the children of Stilicho's household with the accuracy of his missing limb's weather predictions.

"It hurts like thunder. That means we'll have rain later." He surveyed the bloody morning sky. "Aye, red sun in morning means a storm's coming."

Weather! Always a safe topic when you want to cover your feelings. "Rain is our friend today. It will mask our progress and keep the patrols inside their shelters."

"Maybe, but we need no more mud." He knocked a clod off his single boot with his crutch, then looked over his shoulder at Tia. "I'm concerned about the Augusta. She looks so ill. Is this trip wise?"

Placidia told him of the threats she and Manius had heard over the past week. "I think this is the best we can hope for. Tia needs to be away from the court...as do I."

His eyes grew wide, but he didn't question further.

The small caravan formed up, four guards on horseback in front of the wagon pulled by two mules, and four guards behind. Angelus, on foot, headed into the tall weeds on a path only he could see. The sky darkened. She looked up as clouds rolled in to obscure the sun. Soon, a steady drizzle dampened their mood as well as their clothes. A cold breeze made it feel more like late fall than late summer.

Paulus draped a cloak over his head and shoulders. The image of Angelus suffering from the wet and cold in his thin tunic and bare legs crossed her mind. Placidia retreated to the relative dryness of the wagon to look for her spare wool cloak. She found it in the back. The thick brown fibers smelled of sheep. The

25

natural oil of the wool made it nearly waterproof, as well as warm.

She called to the guard riding just behind the wagon, "Tell the captain to bring the boy to me. I have something for him."

The man rode ahead. Within moments the caravan stopped. Manius and the drenched, shivering boy appeared at the wagon.

"You wanted Angelus, Lady?" Manius frowned.

"I can't have my angel catching cold. Take this." Placidia smiled, handing the boy the cloak.

He wrapped himself in the warm wool, pulled a fold up over his sopping hair, and smiled. "Thank you, Princess."

Manius growled at the boy.

"Er, thank you, Lady."

CHAPTER 5

They continued wending their way through the marshes, skirting quiet pools of water birds and muddy bogs. Angelus warned them of hazards: fallen trees and dangerous sinkholes. The cold rain became a light drizzle by late afternoon.

"Whoa!" Paulus called to the mules as a back wheel slid off the narrow track. Placidia grabbed the wagon seat as it shuddered. "Jump off, Princess!"

Blessed Mother Mary, not again! Placidia scrambled over the side onto the track. This was the third time the wagon got stuck. She shivered, pulling her cloak over her head. *Will we ever leave this swamp?*

She helped Tia exit the back of the tilted wagon. They stood waiting on the path as the horses and men pulled the wagon back onto the track with ropes and a good deal of swearing. Mud speckled everyone, from head to toe. Her cousin, pale and listless, huddled against her. *Tia, what have I got you into?* Placidia held her close.

"Angelus!" Placidia called to their guide, who was watching the men labor. The boy turned. "How much further?"

"Not much." He pointed to a trio of bumps on the horizon. "We'll camp there 'til dark."

With the wagon righted, Angelus led them to three hillocks just out of sight of the Roman road in the misty twilight. The small bumps, fuzzed with scrubby trees, barely hid their camp. Placidia peeped over the top of one hill. *Cold camp tonight, but maybe I can light the small brazier in the wagon to heat some broth for Tia. She's getting worse by the hour.*

"Are we out of the swamp yet?" Tia sat up as Placidia entered the back of the wagon.

Placidia pushed her dark feelings away. She had to appear brave for her cousin. "No. We've stopped for a rest and something to eat before crossing the Roman road after dark."

"How much longer?" Her cousin moved restlessly. "I'd like to get out of this stuffy wagon."

"Of course." Placidia helped Tia down and pulled a folding camp stool from the back for her sit on. Doing something helpful—no matter how small—soothed her nerves. Noticing Manius and Angelus talking, she said, "I'll ask the captain how much longer."

"Lady." Manius tipped his head in a slight bow as Placidia joined them. "How does my mistress?"

"Her cough is worse, and she's weaker. Are you sure we cannot take the main roads?"

The captain shook his head. "I have reliable sources that say the roads are infested with so-called bandits, waiting to do Olympius' bidding."

"A sea route would have been much easier on Tia." She left the accusation hanging.

"Olympius expected that. The port is closely watched. All ships leaving are boarded and searched. The Master of Offices does not intend the Augusta to make it to Rome."

Her shoulders slumped. "How much longer in these swamps?"

"Angelus says we should camp until dark. When the moon comes up, we can see to move, and cross the road."

"How much longer after that, Angelus?"

The boy looked into the sky. "If the clouds drift away from the moon, we can move faster. If the rain continues..." he shrugged, "...well after midnight, maybe dawn. If we leave the wagon, we can be out of these marshes by mid-evening."

"The Augusta is too weak to ride a horse or be exposed in a litter." Placidia spared a concerned glance for her cousin, huddled and miserable on the canvas stool. "We must keep the wagon."

"As you will, Lady." Manius took off to supervise the guards making camp.

"How does my angel?" Placidia turned to Angelus, one corner of her mouth lifted in a crooked smile.

"Warm, thanks to you, Lady."

"You look tired." She reached out a hand to push a thatch of hair from his face. *Was there a hint of moisture in his eyes?* The boy blinked, turning away. She knew country children took on adult tasks at a very young age, but Angelus was still only a boy. *Was this journey too for much him?*

"What's wrong, Angelus?"

He took several gulps of air, then glanced at Manius. "It's…my gran, Lady. She's been sickly lately. I took this job to get money for a doctor. She's took with a fever and I had to leave her with a girl from the village. I don't know if she lives or…" He sniffed and straightened, getting control of himself. "Excuse me, Lady, I didn't mean to chatter on so." He turned to walk away.

She placed a hand on his arm. "Angelus, I'm truly sorry about your grandmother. I'll pray for her recovery. No one should be with strangers at the end." They looked toward the wagon as Manius reported to Tia. "When we are through with this, I'll see what I can do for you and your gran."

"Thank you, Lady." He bowed and retreated.

They settled into their cold camp. The horses and mules, freed from their burdens, but not their tack, stamped and snorted, trying to free their legs from clumps of mud and their faces from the biting insects that gathered in still places. Placidia had Paulus light the brazier to heat up meat broth spiced with pepper for Tia, who sipped only a little before retreating to the wagon and falling into a restless sleep. She wasn't the only exhausted one. Placidia saw Angelus drop by one of the hillocks, pull the wool cloak over his head, and not move for over an hour.

"Poor boy. How long has he been awake, after traveling all the night before?" she murmured. She set aside more broth for Angelus, nibbling on olives and cheese for her own meal. Afterwards, Placidia perched on the edge of the wagon, enjoying the setting sun. The rains had moved on; the evening skies cleared. The brazier warmed her back, but they would have to extinguish it as darkness set in.

Manius approached her. "I'll take the boy to check out the Roman road. See how often the patrols ride by. We'll be back by moonrise. I'll have Nepos prepare the camp and repack the wagon."

"Thank you, Captain."

He moved off to confer with his second-in-command.

Placidia heard a rustling by the wagon and saw the boy dawdling by the wheel. "Angelus, up here. I have something for you."

He gave a slight bow. "You should put out the brazier, Lady. Its glow will attract attention."

"We lit it only to heat food for Tia. I'll put it out soon. Did you get anything to eat?"

His stomach growled in response. A blush crept up his cheeks.

"I thought not." She laughed. "Manius forgets you're a growing boy, and hungry all the time." She thrust the warm cup into his hands. "Drink this."

"Thank you, Lady." He sniffed appreciatively, then gulped the bracing brew. He wiped his mouth on the back of his sleeve. "That should warm my bones."

"Here's more—meat, bread, cheese—to tide you over." She handed down a packet she had prepared earlier. He nodded, then turned to go.

"Angelus?"

"Yes?"

"I've been praying for your grandmother." She stared into the lengthening shadows. "Stay safe."

"I will, Lady."

Placidia watched Manius and the boy disappear into the murk. A sudden yawn nearly cracked her face and an overwhelming lethargy weighed down her limbs. She had gotten almost no sleep the night before, and it had been a tiring day. *Better sleep while I can. Who knows when I'll get to rest my head again.*

She crawled into the wagon and promptly dropped into a dreamless sleep next to her cousin.

CHAPTER 6

P rincess! Princess, wake up." Paulus' gruff voice and gentle shaking brought Placidia around.

For a moment, the dark, close quarters confused her. Then the events of the past days crowded back. "I'm awake. Is the captain back?" She sat up. The camp exuded a feeling of purpose and activity in the dark.

Paulus held a faint oil lamp under his chin, giving his face a ghostly appearance. "Yes, he and the lad timed the patrols. We must break down the wagon to get it across the road. I've made a comfortable spot for you and the Augusta while the men work."

"Paulus?" Tia's faint voice came from the other pallet.

"Yes, Augusta. I've warmed some wine for you."

Placidia helped her cousin to the ground and into Paulus' capable hands. "Where's the captain?"

Paulus pointed over his shoulder toward the horses.

She approached Manius and his second-in-command Nepos as they stood talking in muted tones. "What's the plan, Captain? Paulus said we need to break down the wagon?"

"Yes, Princess. We need boards to bridge the ditches to the road. As I thought might happen, Olympius has increased the patrols. We need to be quick and efficient to cross without detection. Everyone must do as required, with as little noise as possible."

"Anything I can do?" Possible danger flooded out the last of her lethargy.

"If you don't mind getting your hands dirty…?"

"You mean dirtier than they already are?" Placidia raised her grimy hands for inspection.

Manius' white teeth flashed in the dark. "We need to cover our faces and any shiny tack with mud, to hide next to the road."

"Of course." She pulled one foot from the muck. "Anything not already covered will be by the time you're done with the wagon."

She helped a pair of guards cover shiny buckles and darken one gray horse's hide, while the rest partially disassembled the wagon. The covering tent came down, a couple of slats from the sides were pried off, and several hampers were removed and strapped to the backs of horses. When they broke camp, Tia returned to a pallet in the back. Placidia joined the men on foot, leading their horses.

Several yards short of the road—she hoped out of eyesight in the shrubby marsh—Manius called a halt. He sent half his men to hide in the ditches with the wagon boards. He motioned to Angelus and a slight-built young soldier—evidently saving the stronger men for pushing the wagon or helping drag it from the mud. "Angelus, you go east toward Ravenna; Silus, west until you're out of sight of the crossing. Give the signal when you're in place. Twice if a patrol approaches. We'll signal back when the wagon starts across the road, and again when it's safely on the other side and you can return. Be quick. The longer we linger by the road, the greater our chances of discovery."

Angelus and the young guard took off in opposite directions along the raised Roman road, ready to dive for a ditch if they heard horses. A full moon, crossed by wispy clouds, rose in the sky. Low mist swirled about their knees. Placidia stood with two horses, a calming hand on their noses to keep them from nickering at any of their fellows that might come down the road.

They heard the signals for patrols and hunkered down, waiting for them to pass. First one from Ravenna, then another shortly after from the opposite direction.

"Now!" Manius hissed. Guards in the ditch put planks across to the road. The remaining soldiers led the horses over the gap and onto the road. Tia, Paulus and Placidia waited behind as the mules hauled the lightened wagon over.

"Our turn, Tia." She helped her cousin across the swaying boards and onto the solid road, followed by the surprisingly agile Paulus.

Once on the road, the guards scrambled to reverse the process on the other side. The boards bridged the other ditch and the horses started across. An owl hoot screeched from the direction of Ravenna. One hoot. One rider. Not a patrol. Placidia's heart raced.

"Princess, you and the Augusta go next." Manius grabbed her elbow, propelling her toward the bridged ditch. "If you have to, don't wait for the wagon, ride!"

"Understood, Captain."

An unearthly howling came echoing over the swamp. Then a riderless horse careened toward the wagon.

"Captain!" Placidia grabbed his arm. "Angelus. Something's wrong."

Manius nodded. "Men! Get that horse. Nepos, get the women to safety." Manius unsheathed his short sword and hurried down the road toward the noise.

"Princess, Augusta, under cover, now!" The young second-in-command hurried the women and Paulus to the edge of the road, over the bridge and down the path, out of sight. "Stay here." He left them by a pool of water with the horses. Tia shivered in Placidia's arms. Her own breath came in rapid pants as she tried to still her racing heart.

Paulus drew his knife and stood by them.

Placidia strained her ears. Three hoots, signaling all were across. The wagon joined them shortly, then the rest of the guards, and the riderless horse.

Two hoots from the west. A patrol! Two guards struggled to control the frightened, riderless horse. The animal rolled its eyes, nickered and reared. One guard loosened his sword. They had to get the horse under control or put it down.

Without thinking, Placidia approached and threw her cloak over the horse's head. It stopped rearing but stood trembling on the path. She placed a soothing hand on its neck, whispering.

She spied Manius and Angelus slipping into the group just as the patrol trotted past. All froze until the sound of hoofbeats vanished. Soon afterwards, Silus, covered in mud, joined them.

"Nice work with the horse, Princess." Manius said in low tones. "Angelus, lead us out of here."

The boy limped past Placidia to head the column. He held his shoulders stiffly, hissing in pain with each step.

"What happened?" She turned to Manius.

"Later, Princess." The captain lifted Tia, then Placidia, into the wagon.

Placidia mumbled, "Who does he think he is, keeping things from me. Angelus needs help!"

"What?" Tia murmured from her pallet.

"Nothing, Sweeting. Go to sleep. We'll be out of the swamp by dawn." Placidia blushed as she realized her hypocrisy in keeping things from Tia. The captain was only looking out for her welfare. They couldn't stop until they were well away from the Roman road.

The wagon joined the small single file caravan on its march through the remaining marshes. After an hour of trudging, the moon set. Angelus called a halt in a meadow surrounded by willow thickets. As the horses and mules grazed, the men sat in tired groups, sipping from flasks, exchanging the occasional grunt.

Placidia jumped out of the wagon to seek out Manius. "Now, Captain. Who is the horse's rider? What's wrong with Angelus?"

"The horse's rider is—was an imperial messenger. I have his satchel here." He patted a mud-spattered leather courier bag slung over his shoulder. "Angelus thought to delay him by playing the madman, but evidently the courier thought him more likely a thief and attacked the lad with his whip."

"And you had to let the boy lead us for an hour without attending his wounds." Placidia said, sorrowful at the needful neglect.

"Angelus is of sturdy stock, and our priority is the Augusta's and your safety. We needed to get away from the road, and he is our guide." Manius ran a grimy hand through his hair. "We'll stay here until dawn to rest and reassemble the wagon. Princess." He bowed, then left to rouse his men.

Only with the flare of a torch did she notice the dark stains on the front of his uniform.

"ANGELUS?" PLACIDIA STOOD OVER THE BOY with a tray of medicines and bandages. He looked so small and helpless, sleeping on the ground. His face was swollen, and she spied bloody stripes on his neck and hands. He must still be in pain. It's a wonder he can sleep. He blinked up at her in the light of an oil lamp. "I heard what you did on the road. You're a brave boy."

"Or a stupid one. I'm not sure which." He sat up and yawned.

"Maybe both?" She laughed and put the tray down. "Let me see to those wounds."

He dropped the cloak and pulled his tunic over his head, hissing as dried blood pulled at the whip marks. He stood, shivering in a ragged loincloth that barely afforded him modesty. She clucked in sympathy. "This will hurt."

He stifled a moan as she cleaned the wounds on his neck and face with diluted wine. She examined the bruises on his belly and back, then wound his body with linen cloths. "I wish I had some arnica," she muttered while she worked. "Here. Wear this under your tunic; it will shield the open wounds from the coarser material." She handed him a silk tunica.

He fondled it gently, then handed it back. "I can't take this, Lady. It's much too fine."

"Nothing is too fine for my angel. Let me help you put it on." She tugged the tunica, then his own rough garment, over his head and pulled his arms through, eliciting only a couple hisses of pain.

"Thank you, Lady. I'll give it to Gran when I get home. She deserves such fine stuff. I'll only get it dirty and stained. Gran…" His words choked off, eyes glittering with tears in the lamplight. He closed them so as not to cry in front of her. A single tear rolled down his cheek.

She reached out to gently brush it away. The boy sobbed.

"It's all right, Angelus." She embraced him lightly, trying to be considerate of his bruises.

He stiffened, keeping his crying to a couple of suppressed hiccups and swallowing his tears. "Thank you, Lady, for your comfort and kind words."

She dropped her arms, nodding. *He's a boy doing a man's work. I need to be careful of his pride.*

He scanned the eastern horizon. "No sign of dawn. It'll be several more hours before we're out of here and I can go home."

Placidia patted his hand. "I know you're worried. You will be with your gran soon."

He nodded. His stomach growled. "Can we get a bite while the wagon's being rebuilt?"

"Of course." She smiled. "Then you rest."

*****

35

PLACIDIA GROANED AS SHE SLID FROM THE MESSENGER HORSE'S SADDLE, THEN stood holding onto the girth. *Blessed Mother of God, how long has it been since I've ridden so long? Even my teeth ache. I'll be stiff tomorrow.*

By noon they had left the worst of the marshes behind and ascended to a solid wind-swept land dotted with sheep and goats. The caravan pulled into a small copse of willow trees by a meandering creek that drained into the marsh. They were north and west of the city, only a few miles as the bird flies, but had traversed many more. A journey that should have ended well before dusk the day it began had taken three times as long.

"I know," Placidia murmured to the horse. "All you want is a soft bed of straw and a good rub down. Me, too." She gave the horse to a tired looking guard, who led it to the herd grazing beside the stream. He removed the tack and started rubbing the horse down with a wool cloth. "Ha! You got yours before I got mine." Placidia chuckled. "Lucky boy."

Making her way to the wagon to check on Tia, she noticed Manius conferring with Angelus. The boy pointed over a low hill. The captain handed him a small bag. As she approached, Manius said, "I don't know when, or if, I'll be back... tell Marta, when you see her..." He looked wistfully over his shoulder in the direction of Ravenna, then shook his head. "Better not to make promises I might not be able to keep." He reached down to clasp the boy's forearm like a man. "You're a good lad."

Angelus smiled and turned to go.

"Angelus!" Placidia called. She couldn't let the boy leave without showing her own gratitude

He walked stiffly to the wagon.

"Thank you for getting us through the marsh. I know your heart was elsewhere, and you sacrificed much to save us." She dug into the coin purse hanging from her belt, handed him two gold solidi—more money than he would see in years of toil—and kissed him lightly on the cheek.

His face burned as he handed the coins back. "Thank you, Lady, but I'm too poor for gold. If I tried to spend it, I'd likely be branded a thief. Who would care for Gran then?"

"A smart boy, as well as brave. Wait a moment." She climbed into the wagon, rummaged in a box, and handed him a clinking sack. "Here, take silver and bronze instead."

"Many thanks, Lady Who Is Not a Princess. If you ever need to get back into the city quiet-like, through the marsh, ask around for me. I'll get the word."

"I'd trust no other."

He grinned, bowed, and disappeared into the bracken.

Paulus, sitting quietly on the wagon seat during the whole exchange, grunted. "Wasted good coin on that lad. Likely, he'll spend it on sweets or wine. His gran will see none of it."

"Perhaps, but I have a feeling I'll see our Angel of the Marshes again someday."

CHAPTER 7

Apennine Mountain Pass, early September 408

Things will be rougher in these mountains." Paulus shaded his eyes as he surveyed the switch-back paths tracking up the rising slopes. "Wish we could take the good Roman roads."

"Me, too." Placidia sighed. "Maybe on the other side." She shifted on the hard seat to look back through the wagon at the messenger's horse on a lead. She had worked out the stiffness during the past five days of riding along the eastern side of the Apennines. Now it was time to cross. *Good mount. Lots of stamina. Easier to ride him than sit on this damned wooden seat. No, let the horse rest. We may need a spare mount if a horse takes a sprain on those jagged peaks.*

Halfway through the afternoon, Placidia noticed a commotion with the forward guard. Her heart raced as Manius cried, "Bandits! Form up!"

A small band of men in mismatched Roman armor streamed out of a side ravine. With barbarian screams, their assailants threw themselves on the guards, who beat the men back.

"In the back, Princess!" Paulus pushed Placidia into the wagon. Muddled shouts and the clash of arms surrounded them as she grabbed Tia and huddled in the wagon. Her mouth dried with fear. *Were these the bandits from Olympius come to kill Tia?*

"Manius! I know one o' them." Paulus' gruff voice called out. "Gainus! Halt your attack. It's Paulus of Stilicho's household."

The sounds of battle ceased. Placidia peeked out the front. These men didn't

38

look like well-fed agents masquerading as bandits. They were half-starved, sporting old wounds and battered armor.

A short, powerful-looking man with a red beard stepped forward. "Paulus? Are you fleeing the massacres? If so, you're going the wrong way. King Alaric is in the north."

"What massacres?" Manius edged his mount forward, sword at the ready.

"All across the land, for the last two days. After Honorius…" many men spat at the mention of her brother's name "…had Stilicho executed, the Roman legions had orders to expel the barbarian auxiliaries. They butchered us. Thousands dead."

Another man, with a bloody bandage covering one eye, spoke with venom. "The bastards murdered our wives and babes. Herded them into our churches and burned them, saying they had to exterminate Arian heretics."

Placidia gasped. Olympius had used religion as an excuse for his barbarian purge! Her father had banned Arianism, the belief that Christ the Son was separate from and less than God the Father, but emperors had always turned a blind eye to variations in Christian belief in the army. How could Honorius sanction this terrible deed against innocent women and children, much less gut his army with enemies on his borders?

"If you're not going to join King Alaric, what are you doing on the road with a wagon and armed men?" Gainus asked. "Who's in the wagon, Paulus?"

Tia's guards pulled closer to the wagon with their horses and naked swords.

"Captain, I believe we can trust these men," Paulus said in low tones. "Gainus served in Stilicho's personal army."

"I know the man." Tia's soft voice came from behind Placidia. "Ask him about my brother."

"What of young Eucherius?" Paulus asked. "I watched Stilicho butchered from the church door, but have heard nothing of his son."

"I was one of a dozen men entrusted to take Eucherius to Rome and his mother. We were on the road only two days when the order came down from the emperor for Eucherius' execution on charges of treason. We took to the back roads, made it to Rome. He went into sanctuary at St. Paul's. Rome is no longer safe for us, so we're looking to join King Alaric." Gainus stared again at the wagon. "I'll ask one more time, Paulus: who is in the wagon?"

Tia crawled to the front, parted the curtain, then stood behind Paulus. Placidia had never seen her frail cousin act so brave. Tia held her head high.

There was the ring of command in her voice. "I am Thermantia, former Augusta, daughter of General Stilicho. I travel with my maid and my guard to Rome and my mother. Why do you attack my company?"

Manius shielded her. "Be wary, Augusta."

Tia put a reassuring hand on his shoulder. "They are my father's soldiers, Captain. They will not harm me."

Manius kept his horse next to the wagon and did not sheath his sword.

Gainus' men murmured among themselves. Heads nodded in recognition.

"I am Gainus, Augusta, late a centurion in your father's Gothic troop." He bowed briefly. "We did not know it was you. We journey to join King Alaric's forces."

"I heard your stories of massacres." Her voice trembled with emotion. "My heart goes out to you and your families. I too have suffered a terrible loss. You are welcome to join our camp tonight. Anything I can do to help you on your way, I will."

"Thank you, Augusta." Gainus bowed. "We are hungry and weary. Food and company for the night will be appreciated."

"Captain, make it so." Tia crawled back into the wagon as it lurched forward in search of a more likely camping spot. She tumbled to her knees, then sat on the pallet, trembling.

Placidia folded her in her arms. "That was brave. Your father would be proud."

Tia shook her head. "What has Honorius done? Innocent women and children burned in their churches. Loyal soldiers killed in their beds."

"Not Honorius. This is Olympius' work." Placidia patted Tia's hair.

"Do not defend him." Her cousin stiffened and pushed her away. "It might be Olympius whispering in his ear, but Honorius is emperor. It all lands at his feet, and he will pay for it."

"Of course, Tia. I only meant…"

"I don't care." Tears trembled in her eyes. "My father is dead, my brother accused of treason. How long before they lure Eucherius out of sanctuary and butcher him, too?"

"I'm sorry, Tia! If I could change things, I would!"

"I know. I'm just so tired…the danger…the travel…I want my mother!" Tia collapsed onto the pallet and started coughing into a linen kerchief.

Placidia gave her medicine and replaced the blood-stained kerchief.

*****

"More wine, Captain?" Manius' eyes widened as Placidia poured the drink into his tin cup. "My mistress has retired for the night, and I thought you might like a final drink before I join her." She schooled her face into a neutral smile as a thrill of excitement prickled her skin. With her servant's clothes and the deep night shadows, she pulled off her deception as imperial servant. Those guards not on duty, along with most of the barbarians, slept in their bedrolls. Only Manius, Paulus, and Gainas still huddled by a small fire, discussing the hazards before them.

"Thanks, girl," Gainas grunted. "I could use a final draft. We've got hard riding for the next few days if we want to catch up to King Alaric and his army." He took a gulp. "Good stuff! Don't know as when we'll get such as this again."

Paulus gave her a warning look as she poured a drink for him. She shifted back to the shadows with her pitcher to listen as he asked, "Where's Alaric? What are his plans?"

"He's gathering the expelled barbarian units in the north, in the Po valley." Gainas chuckled. "That bastard Honorius will rue the day he butchered our families and sent us into the arms of a great general. Alaric is trained in Roman fighting. He'll lead us well."

"Do you think Alaric will attack Ravenna?" Manius looked over the rim of his cup, concern in his eyes. "It's near impregnable."

Gainas slapped a biting insect from his leg. "I don't know what Alaric will do. He negotiated with Stilicho, but with him dead, it's anybody's guess. I only know what I want, and that's to kill as many Romans as I can."

Placidia took in a sharp breath. *Oh, Honorius, if you could only see what your rash actions have brought. War? Siege? Vengeful barbarians destroying farms and villages? This didn't have to be!* Regret tinged with anger roiled her stomach.

Manius sat up straighter and put his cup to the side, freeing his hand to hover over his knife.

Gainas spluttered, "Not your company, Captain! I'd never harm another in service to Stilicho's family."

Manius relaxed—slightly. "Any trouble on the road from Rome? We hope to get the Augusta there as quietly as possible."

Placidia listened eagerly as the trio discussed the hazards ahead. When the conversation turned to war stories, she stowed her pitcher and crawled into the

41

wagon. Burrowing under the covers on her pallet, she smiled as she drifted off to sleep. *Soon we'll be in Rome. Serena. Older. Wiser in the ways of the court. We'll be safe there with Aunt Serena. She'll know what to do. How to handle Honorius…*

CHAPTER 8

Outside the gates of Rome, late September 408

Good riddance!" Placidia cried as Paulus drove the wagon off to sell it. He would pay for a ride into Rome on a merchant's cart later.

"What?" Tia smiled. "You're happy to give up the smells and fleas?"

Despite their best efforts to stay clean on the nineteen-day journey, the wagon smelled of unwashed bodies and stale food. They had avoided inns and camped the entire way, eating wild game and buying food from local markets. Here, within sight of the walls of Rome, they stabled their horses and purchased a covered litter.

"More than happy!" Placidia plaited Tia's greasy hair and slapped road dust out of their clothes.

Tia offered Placidia a small, stoppered vial. "Try this."

She sniffed. "Oil of roses! Thanks, cousin." Placidia rubbed a bit on her wrists and neck, but it did little to hide her stench. She longed for a hot bath with the passion she normally reserved for riding.

Manius approached with four of his beefiest guards carrying the litter. Slender Silas pulled a two-wheeled hand cart piled with their remaining meager possessions.

"It's time, Mistress." Manius helped Tia into the litter and closed the curtains. Placidia took her proper servant place—on foot, alongside the litter. The guards hoisted the contraption to their shoulders with grunts. Two remaining guards trailed the cart, while Manius led the small company south for Rome on the Via Flaminia.

As they approached the walls, traffic slowed to a crawl.

"What's happening?" Tia peeked out from behind her curtains. "Oh!"

Merchants and farmers leading carts with their wares. Laborers with tools on their backs and families in tow. Scattered nobles in litters like their own, surrounded by servants. All clogged the road.

"Why is everyone fleeing to the city?" Placidia asked Manius.

"I don't know. I'll find out." The captain waded into the crowd to approach a prosperous-looking merchant. Placidia watched in concern as the merchant flailed his arms in agitation. Manius nodded grimly and returned.

"King Alaric passed by Ravenna and is marching on the more vulnerable Rome. Everyone for miles around is headed into the city hoping to be safe behind its walls."

"At least we won't be closely inspected." Placidia nodded toward the gate where harried guards herded the crowd through as fast as they could. She had feared they might be stopped or recognized, but the gatekeepers didn't give them a glance—just another well-to-do lady and her personal guard escaping into the city.

We're here! A thrill shivered up Placidia's spine as they passed by the stout gates and through the tunnel piercing the deep walls. Home. Safety. Rome.

Manius formed the troop into a wedge to lead them through crooked streets packed with people seeking shelter. They jostled their way to the bottom of the Caelian Hill. The litter tilted as they started up the steep street to the lavish mansion Serena maintained near the top.

Tia pulled the curtains back, grinning. "We're nearly there, Placidia!" A little color showed on her cousin's cheeks. "We made it!"

"Not without considerable help and luck." Placidia ticked off her fingers. "We have our angel of the marshes, our stout company, and brave captain to thank. Do you know anything of the captain's personal life?"

"No. Why do you ask?" Tia leaned forward, curiosity animating her face.

"I think he has a relationship with a cook—Marta?—in the Ravenna palace. She's Angelus' cousin. Manius seemed torn at having to leave her for service in Rome. He's a good and loyal man. He deserves some consideration when we're settled."

"Of course. I'll bring it up with Mother."

They lapsed into a satisfied silence. Placidia felt herself relax as they grew closer to the safety of Serena's home. Although raised in an imperial household, she had not realized how burdensome responsibility could be. She might have some small sympathy for her brother carrying the weight of an empire…if he did the work.

The litter stopped outside a high-walled compound. Placidia watched Manius pound on the brass-bound wooden gate.

There was no response.

"Open for the daughter of the house," Manius shouted. He banged the door harder. "We bring Lady Thermantia home to her mother."

A bald brown head appeared over the wall, surveying the small party.

Tia stepped out of the litter. "Peter, let us in. Don't make us dawdle in the street."

"Of course, Mistress." Peter smiled, then shouted to servants they couldn't see. "Open the gates, you laggards. Our young mistress is home!"

As Placidia passed through the gates, into the atrium, she was struck with a sense of unease. She had expected happy faces and a warm welcome, but some servants were tearful. Others engaged in angry conversations in corners, frowning, waving their arms. She glanced at her cousin.

Tia's smile faded into a worried frown. "Peter, what's wrong? Where's Mother?"

The servant's gaze shifted from her cousin's face to the ground. "She's in the solar, Mistress. You should go to her."

Tia lifted her skirts and took off at a sprint. Within ten paces she stopped, doubled over, and gave way to chest-tearing coughs. Placidia joined her, then turned to Manius.

"Captain, settle your men. Peter will show you where. I'll take Lady Thermantia to her mother and check back with you soon." Placidia took Tia's arm and supported her through the receiving room, past the formal dining triclinium, and under the shaded colonnade enclosing the interior garden. At the far end, the solar door stood open.

They found Serena sitting on a blue silk-cushioned bench, staring at her hands, silent tears rolling down her cheeks. She had aged ten years in the year since Placidia had last seen her. Gray streaked her dark hair; the lines on her face were deeply etched. Loose skin hung from her arms where she had lost weight.

"Mother!" Tia cried, racing to her side.

"Tia?" Serena, a dazed expression on her face, clasped her daughter to her breast. "Oh, thank the Good Lord. I thought you dead."

"Is that why you mourn?" Tia wiped the tears from her mother's cheeks. "I'm here, safe with Placidia. We escaped Ravenna and that vile Olympius and had such adventures along the way!" Two hectic red spots bloomed on Tia's cheeks, then faded as her mother broke into fresh tears.

Placidia took a seat on the other side of Serena. "What is it, Aunt?"

"We just got word. My son is dead."

"Eucherius? We heard he was in sanctuary." Placidia's throat closed with her own tears for the gentle boy she grew up with.

Serena stiffened. Her face took on an implacable look, reminding Placidia of the formidable woman who had raised her. "He was betrayed by one of his own men. Like Judas, the betrayer took silver to convince Eucherius he could get him safely from Rome to our relatives in Spain. Honorius' executioners waited outside the church and struck immediately." Her shoulders shook with suppressed sobs. "They won't even give me his body for Christian burial."

Tia collapsed, sobbing, in her mother's lap. Serena absently stroked her daughter's hair. "Tia, my dove, we must put on a brave face. We can't let the world know how much we suffer. We are imperial women." Serena reached around Placidia's shoulder to pull her close. "We are Theodosians."

As proud as Placidia was of her lineage, she wasn't sure a name would keep her safe in these troubled times. For now, she took comfort in her aunt's embrace. *We'll mourn today and face the world tomorrow—together.*

"WHY CAN'T STAY I WITH YOU?" Placidia cried as the shock of abandonment rippled through her body. After a week of feeling safe and cared for again, Serena asked that she leave. "I had nothing to do with Honorius. I tried to turn him away from this course!"

"I know." Serena put a hand to Placidia's face. "My beloved husband and son are dead. My last child is dying. You are all that is left to me, and I must give you up to save you."

"Tia is stronger than you think. With time and nursing…" Placidia's words trailed off at a pitying look from her aunt.

"You and I know she has the same wasting disease that killed her sister. All our prayers, love, and the agency of the best imperial physicians could not save Maria, and they will not save Tia. I will not stay long in this world after she has left it."

"But you have me, Aunt. I love you like a mother, and will care for you if you let me. This separation is not necessary."

A sad smile flickered across Serena's face. "My dear, you are still so young. Olympius' faction is nearly as strong here as at court, and I am tainted through my marriage. Panic is spreading among the people of Rome. I've already heard rumors that I favor the barbarians and might betray the city. It's dangerous for you to be in any way attached to me. Honorius may not sanction my murder, but Olympius reigns. He is determined to wipe out any who might be a rival influence with your brother."

"I would never let them hurt you." Placidia recognized the powerlessness of her words. "I can't lose you, too! You're the only one left I care about."

"Placidia, you must leave and not visit." Serena sighed. "I will put it about that we quarreled over Honorius' actions. You must repudiate me and Tia. Retire to a quiet life at the palace, or better yet one of your estates far outside the city."

"I cannot abandon you. You are my only family."

Serena gripped Placidia's arms tightly. "You must promise me this. I will not be responsible for your death. I might weather this storm and we can be reunited, but if I am accused, you must save yourself, Placidia. Do not put yourself in peril; do not raise your hand to save me. I could not bear to think I would be the instrument of any harm to you." Serena pulled her into a final hug and whispered, "Now go, and do not come back until I say it is safe. I'll send Paulus, Manius, and his guards with you."

Placidia, a knot of tears choking her voice, nodded, leaving the comfort of Serena's arms.

As the litter carried her to the imperial palace, she looked back on her aunt's home and whispered, "God save you, if I cannot."

PART II

THE SEIGE

OCTOBER 408 - JANUARY 409

CHAPTER 9

Imperial Palace, Rome, October 408

W hat can I do for you, Prefect?" Placidia asked as the servant poured
wine in an azure glass goblet.

Since her arrival at the Imperial Palace two weeks earlier, she
had entertained a steady stream of distinguished Roman visitors—senators,
churchmen, businessmen—all seeking her influence with her brother on their
behalf. She did not disabuse them of the notion she *had* influence, as they kept
her in touch with the rapidly changing political climate. Priscus Attalus, the
city's prefect, was one of her favorite visitors.

A man of medium height, with graying dark curls, the prefect turned from
admiring an antique marble bust of Athena. "This is a lovely piece. A copy of
the original by the Greek master Phidias, is it not? I admire his work and have
several reproductions myself."

"I am far from an expert on art."

"Then let me be your teacher." Attalus approached, taking his wine from the
offered silver tray. "I am known for my expertise in these matters."

"I would be delighted to have you tutor me in the arts, Prefect, but it is
my understanding there are more pressing issues we should address." Placidia
smiled to take the sting out of her rebuke. She normally enjoyed flirting with
the charming prefect, but she had heard disturbing rumors and wanted to get
to the point.

"Some other time then, Princess." Attalus, obviously disappointed, turned to the point of his visit. "After the barbarians bypassed Ravenna and moved on Rome, it is rumored Emperor Honorius asked your nephew, Emperor Theodosius II, for troops to protect him from Alaric."

"I have no knowledge of that. Given that my brother, in his wisdom, chose to destroy a third of his army and humiliate a powerful general who could have protected our borders, it does not surprise me he would turn to the East." Placidia took a sip of her own wine. *How much should I tell the good Prefect about our family squabbles? I trust him more than the other bureaucrats, but...* She shrugged. "It was a great blow to the empire when my older brother Arcadius died in May, leaving a seven-year-old boy to rule. If my nephew's regent sees Rome threatened, I'm sure the East will send troops. Uncle Stilicho had a lot of respect for the man."

"The request was for Ravenna's protection. Your brother has refused to send soldiers to Rome."

Placidia kept her face impassive, still judging the prefect. "Ravenna is well protected by marsh from the land side, and with naval units from the seaside. Why would Honorius deny Rome the protection of troops?"

"I was hoping you could tell me, Princess." Attalus set aside his wine and leaned toward her. "Would a personal appeal from his sister overcome his reluctance, or should I be making alternate preparations?"

And here it is. Should I tell him of our rift? Lose the advantage of my seeming influence? Can I, in good conscience, not tell him? Attalus should have as much information as he can if he is to defend Rome. Placidia sighed. "It is always better to speak in person with the emperor. He is sometimes...vulnerable...to personal persuasion. But he is also very fearful. He will likely keep the troops at our expense, whether I appeal to him or not."

"I had hoped for better from our emperor." A worried frown marred the prefect's handsome face. He rose. "I am sorry to cut our delightful visit short, Princess, but your assessment means I have much work to do. Rome's walls are strong, but if the barbarians cut off our access to Portus and the grain from Africa, we starve."

"I'm sorry I could not provide more encouragement, Prefect. If you send a delegation, I will add my own written appeal to yours, but I have little hope it will help."

"Would you not be more persuasive in person, Princess? I cannot guarantee your safety if the Goths attack Rome. You would be much safer in Ravenna."

Placidia weighed her answer carefully. She needed allies, and believed Attalus could be one. "Thank you for your concern, Prefect, but I am much safer here than at my brother's court."

He raised his eyebrows but did not pursue the topic. "Thank you for any help you might provide, Princess." Attalus bowed over Placidia's hand.

"What small service I can take in our cause, I will." Placidia rose to escort him to the door of her audience chamber.

Once the prefect left, Placidia slumped. She was weary, worried, and hungry. The wine sat uneasily in her stomach. She turned to her servant. "Get me Paulus." She had installed the elderly veteran as chamberlain of her residence. As she had suspected he would, Honorius held back her servants and possessions. However, she had her own revenues from her father's inheritance, and had established a small but comfortable household in one wing of the Imperial Palace on the Palatine Hill.

Paulus hobbled into view.

"Tell Cook I want a light meal, and tell my maid to prepare a bath."

Studying her face, Paulus asked, "Bad news, Princess?"

"Likely we will be facing Alaric's army without one of our own." She rubbed the back of her neck, futilely trying to relieve the tension. "Paulus, do not spread this news among the household. Panic will come soon enough, without our aiding its arrival."

"Yes, mistress. I'll tell Cook and your maid your wishes, and no more."

"THE BARBARIANS ARE HERE!"

The cries rang through the streets, reaching Placidia's ears only seconds before Paulus came to the entry of the garden to make the announcement himself. It was early morning, and the late October sun had not yet burned the dew from the fragrant rosemary bushes.

She had known of Alaric's approach for days. The city leaders had moved grain from the warehouses in Portus to Rome, a volunteer militia supplemented the city vagiles to maintain order, the churches prepared to distribute food and medicine. All this happened while she sat aloof and helpless in her palace. The city was as ready as it could be without an offensive force to drive the barbarians away from the walls.

"Where are they?" Placidia asked.

"They're occupying the plains outside the walls to the northeast, blocking all bridges and gates, cutting off boat traffic on the Tiber to Portus. I've heard that Alaric seeks negotiation."

"Alaric seeks recognition. He has shown his military prowess repeatedly, but stiff-necked Romans seem incapable of giving the man the respect and honors that would placate him." She looked around the garden and the small corner of peace it represented, then straightened her shoulders. "Assemble the household. I will tell them what to expect."

"As you command, Mistress."

CHAPTER 10

L ater that day, Priscus Attalus, flanked by his personal guard, wended his way through the narrow streets of Rome, toward the Forum and the Curia Julia, better known as the Senate House. He normally loved strolling the streets, talking with ordinary people in the markets. Rome was his home. He loved the monumental aspect of the city, the energy and bustle of its inhabitants, but he couldn't shake the feeling of Rome's decline and decay.

"Jupiter's balls!" Attalus cursed as he stumbled on a loose paving stone. One of his guards stifled a chuckle when he glared at him. Road maintenance—another victim of reduced population and fewer taxes. With the Western emperor in Ravenna and the Eastern emperor in Constantinople, Rome no longer seemed the center of the world. It sheltered nearly 800,000 souls, many fewer than at the height of its glory. *The city's dying,* he thought as he surveyed empty tenement buildings and closed shops. *Better a slow withering away, or a quick death by barbarian fire?*

Attalus shook off his gloomy thoughts as he approached the Senate House. A large crowd gathered outside the modest building. Rival factions shouted in a confused roar:

"Pay off the barbarians!"

"Send the bastards packing!"

"Peace for the people!"

"Rome is great! No surrender!"

Attalus easily spotted the agents leading the chants. Rich people paying crowds to voice their support or opposition was an ancient tradition in Rome.

Attalus and his escort passed through a ring of vigiles guarding the Senate House and and up the steps to an open colonnade where small knots of senators lobbied one another before entering the sacred space. "Join the vigiles," he dismissed his guards. "Arrest anyone who gets too rowdy. I don't want a riot. It might influence our delicate elders to a wrong conclusion."

"Yes, Prefect." His captain deployed the guard. In the face of so many armed men, the crowd already seemed less antagonistic, the chants more rote.

He spotted an ally and waved him over. "Theonas, my friend!" Attalus draped an arm over the shorter man's shoulders. "How are you disposed on the barbarian's demands?"

"Lobbying already, Attalus?" He laughed. "I haven't heard the arguments yet."

"But you've formed an opinion?" Attalus dropped his arm and his smile. "Alaric asks for little compared to the damage he could do. I had hoped you might lead the opposition to Lampadius. He is sure to agitate for war."

"I'm your man, Prefect. Lampadius is of the same ilk as those idiots who advise the emperor. They will ruin us all."

"Thank you, my friend!" Attalus clapped him on the back. "I had to be sure of at least one level head in there."

"I'm not the only one." Theonas looked around the colonnade, then dropped his voice. "But I think we're in the minority."

"We'll see when the vote is taken."

Attalus nodded to two attendants who stood with ceremonial spears outside the imposing brass doors of the Senate. They pounded their spear butts on the marble floor and pushed open the doors, signaling the senate was open for business. Attalus brandished his staff of office as he led the procession into the building. A small thrill of awe tingled his spine. *I never tire of this space. The majesty, the history. All the great men who served here: Caesar, Cicero, Augustus, Seneca, Hadrian...they would be so disappointed in our current crop of leaders.*

The slap of sandals echoed off the marble-clad walls that soared two stories high. Windows near the ceiling let in light and air. Attalus traversed the red and green marble floor of the rectangular interior, passing the opposite ranks of white marble steps that graced the long sides of the building. The steps could accommodate about three hundred seated senators. Today, the senate would be lucky to muster half that number. As the senior imperial official in Rome, he took his place beside the empty throne-like chair at the far end of the room symbolizing the absent emperor.

He turned to watch the senators take their places on the steps, strictly according to rank: the most senior senators with the most honors and offices in front; the least honored took the back benches. Most brought cushions to save their soft asses from the hard marble.

And now for my least favorite part of the ceremony… "Senators, representing our absent Pope Innocent, Bishop Joseph will bless our deliberations." Attalus respectfully bowed his head during the blessing, despite his objections to the Christian faith. At the end, he glanced at the empty spot where the glorious statue of Victory striding the world used to grace the hall and sighed.

Attalus stepped forward, banged his staff on the floor, and cried out in a deep, mellifluous voice that carried to all corners of the building, "Senators! We have a decision to make for our fair city. King Alaric's troops have laid siege to Rome. Do we negotiate?"

A tall distinguished-looking man rose: Lampadius led the anti-barbarian faction in the senate. "I wish to address the august body of the senate of Rome."

"Granted." Attalus nodded.

Lampadius strode to the floor, adjusting his perfectly draped, purple-edged toga. "Friends and fellow Conscript Fathers. It has been over seven hundred years since the barbarians of the north last breached the mighty walls of Rome. Since that time, we have conquered the known world and made those barbarians pay a hundred-thousand-fold for their ancestor's audacity. We cannot let our proud city bow before a barbarian and thief. We should throw his demands back in his face and tell him 'Be gone!' God and right are on our side."

Shouts in favor rose from the senators. *He's a pompous fool but knows how to appeal to this crowd. I doubt the people outside feel the same. Pride doesn't feed children or put a roof over your head.*

Lampadius struck a dramatic pose as he continued extolling the past triumphs of Rome, then returned to his seat amid loud praise from his followers. A smaller cohort, in opposition, shouted for attention.

"I recognize the distinguished Conscript Father Theonas." Attalus nodded as his friend took the center of the floor.

Unlike the high rhetorical style of Lampadius, Theonas addressed the senators with the warmth and common sense of a concerned uncle. "With all deference to my good colleague Lampadius, I feel his approach is wrong-headed. He speaks of the glory days of Rome as if we still had legions of loyal soldiers guarding our borders and our gates. We do not! How did Alaric even make it to our walls in the heart of our empire? Our army is in disarray! We hide behind walls manned by maimed veterans and young boys. When they are overrun, do our wives and daughters take up arms?"

Mutters and confused looks rippled across the senate, giving Attalus hope. *Maybe Theonas can do it. Maybe they'll listen to reason.* The anti-barbarian faction crossed their arms, glaring at being faced with reality.

"It is fall," Theonas continued. "Alaric's people will take our harvests and the grain from Africa. They will feast while our children starve. I say, pay the barbarian the four thousand pounds of gold Stilicho promised, grant him the title he wants, and be glad the price isn't in lives and misery!"

Attalus despaired as a roar of dissent rolled from one end of the chamber to the other. A small minority tried supporting Theonas, but were shouted down. *Damn Lampadius for a hide-bound idiot! His faction will be the death of this city!*

"Order! Order!" Attalus shouted. "All will be heard!"

He eventually imposed order, and the debate continued. Senator after senator affirmed that the walls were strong, the barbarians knew little of siege warfare, the Roman people were brave. Occasionally the opposition made the legal point that the senate had no authority to grant the title and land Alaric wanted without the emperor's permission.

Attalus knew the outcome before he ordered the vote. "Those in favor of negotiating with Alaric to my right. Those opposed to my left." The senators left their seats to array themselves on opposites sides of the room. A far smaller group stood to his right. "Those opposed to negotiating win the vote. The question is answered—"

Lampadius interrupted. "Prefect, there is another issue we should address. May I take the floor?"

He won! What is he up to now? Attalus struggled for an excuse to deny Lampadius' request, but could not find one. "Senators, take your seats."

They shuffled back to their original places, muttering to their friends and glancing at Lampadius. He stood. "Fellow Senators, it is not enough that our walls are thick, and our will is strong. The barbarians have succeeded in taking cities by treachery. We must purge our population of those sympathetic to the Arian horde."

Murmurs of agreement echoed around the room.

Lampadius took a deep breath, then thundered, "Chief among those is the widow of the traitor Stilicho!"

A collective gasp from the senators ended in silence. Attalus stood in stunned disbelief. *Surely someone will come to Lady Serena's aid!*

Lampadius continued. "Her husband made infamous concessions to the so-called Gothic king. Which, you will remember, I stoutly opposed. What is to prevent Lady Serena from opening the gates and allowing the ravenous horde to descend upon our heads? We must rid ourselves of this menace within as we would cut off a putrid limb. She's a traitor. I demand her death. When Alaric realizes he has no ally inside Rome, and sees the strength of our will, he will turn tail and leave like the dog he is!"

A confused and fearful babble rose from the senate chamber. As the yammer grew louder, Attalus realized he would have to take the unpopular position and talk some sense into these frightened old men. *The senate is a toothless Roman wolf that choses to mask its impotence with the bluster of pride and the blood of an innocent woman.*

"Conscript Fathers!" Attalus shouted. With quiet restored, he took his place on the floor. "We have no authority to take the life of an imperial family member. Lady Serena is the niece and adopted daughter of the Great Theodosius Augustus. Only our most Gracious Highness Honorius Augustus can condemn his cousin to death, and he has declined to do so. I will not allow a vote on this issue!"

Pandemonium broke out again. Senators shouted, "Traitor!"

"Would you let that barbarian horde through our gates?"

"Shame, Prefect, shame!"

Attalus banged his staff of office on the marble floor, shouting for order again. "Senators! There are alternatives to murder. We can expel Lady Serena from the city." He took a deep breath before putting a more controversial proposal on the floor. "Our own slaves of barbarian origin are by far a greater menace. We can turn over all the barbarian slaves to Alaric. Let him feed them while we live in safety behind our walls."

This suggestion brought renewed furor. The Senators didn't want to give up their property. *Hypocrites! Willing to murder a Roman woman for possible future treachery, while holding on to slaves more likely to betray them. There must be another way to delay Lady Serena's fate.*

"Conscript Fathers! As I said, the senate does not have the authority to execute Lady Serena. Let us petition Honorius Augustus before we make this drastic move. This session is adjourned!"

And may Princess Placidia forgive me.

CHAPTER 11

They are calling for her execution?" Placidia took one look at Attalus' sorrowful face and her heart nearly stopped beating. She glanced around the receiving room, blinking back tears. "Serena warned me this might happen."

"Yes, my dear. I am truly sorry. I know Lady Serena would never betray her city."

"Of course not!" Placidia snapped. "Stilicho did not commit treason, and neither did his son. These lies and accusations against my aunt are unworthy of the senate." The thoughts of her recent losses tightened her chest. She took a deep breath, not wanting to express her sorrow in front of the Prefect. "What is to be done?" she muttered, to herself more than to Attalus.

"I spoke on Lady Serena's behalf, but could not dissuade them." Attalus leaned forward, speaking in hushed tones so as not to be overheard by the omnipresent servants. "I did delay the vote. We have some time."

Glancing at the hovering servants, Placidia ordered, "Serve the wine and refreshments, then leave us."

Once alone, they resumed their conversation.

"Could Serena be persuaded to leave the city and retire to one of her villas, further south?" Placidia mused.

"Not with the siege on. That would be sending King Alaric an imperial hostage." Attalus sipped his wine, then set it aside.

"How could I forget such a factor? If Alaric did give her safe passage, the senate would take it as proof of her conspiracy with the barbarians."

"Could she seek sanctuary?" Attalus frowned in concentration.

"She could, but I doubt she will." Placidia felt increasingly trapped, with no valid course of action in sight. "My cousin Tia is quite ill. Serena fears her last child has little time left, and will not leave her side." She remembered her aunt's sorrowful voice as she predicted she would have little need for life after her daughter died. "She also fears for me, and asked that I not move to help her. But how can I not?"

"Perhaps more pressing matters will take the senate's attention. Since they rejected Alaric's demands, the siege will grow more perilous." Attalus rubbed a hand across his furrowed forehead. "I did remind the senate that only Honorius Augustus could condemn another member of the royal family. I counseled waiting and caution."

"I feel so helpless!" Placidia launched herself from her chair to stride across the room, scuffing the thick wool carpet, absently touching the fine art and polished wood surfaces. "What good are imperial birth, wealth, and position, if I can do nothing to save my family?" She turned to Attalus. "In the end, I'm just a woman. You're a powerful man. Can you help Serena?"

A look of pain pinched his eyes. "Princess, I have some limited resources, which I will use to counteract this proposal. But feelings are running hot in the city. Lampadius and others have tilled their soil well, and mean to harvest death. Their agents are among the poor, agitating as we speak. Once that suspicion is planted in the mob, I cannot root it out. My own life would be forfeit to try."

"I could go to her, take her in."

"No, Princess!" The look of alarm crossing the Prefect's face brought Placidia's wandering to a halt. "You would risk death, as well. Lady Serena has made it known you two are estranged. That is the only thing keeping the wolves from your door."

"I must do something!" Hot tears rolled down her cheeks. She didn't care if the Prefect saw.

Attalus gathered her into his arms, soothing her sobs with soft words. "Do what Serena—what any mother—would want you to do. My dear, you are what—twenty years old? You put too great a burden on yourself. Serena would want you to live and be happy. You cannot save her and, by trying, you put your life at risk."

Placidia stood still a moment, trying to control her tears. Gradually her breathing grew less labored. She pushed away from Attalus, wiping her eyes. "I am embarrassed at my behavior, Prefect. First accusing you of inaction, then soaking your tunic with my tears. I don't know what you think of me."

"Call me Attalus, and I will think of you as a friend, if you will have me." His face sobered. "This is a challenging time for all of us. Treachery and fear rule men's hearts. It is best to make allies where one can. You are in great danger. You should keep quiet, make no public statements or appearances until this crisis is over."

She nodded, still stunned at her own loss of control. *With Serena banned to me, I have no one in which to confide! No friends. No family. Attalus offers his friendship. Perhaps I should take a chance.* She struggled to control her voice. "Thank you, Pre...uh...Attalus. I value your friendship and counsel. Please keep me apprised of any changes." She extended her hand.

He took the broad hint, bowed over her hand, and excused himself, leaving Placidia to brood over her aunt's fate...and possibly her own.

THE FOLLOWING DAY, Placidia's own restless nature betrayed her when she had to keep to her apartments. At mid-morning she called for Captain Manius to meet her in the atrium, dressed in ordinary clothes rather than his imperial livery.

"Princess?" The captain's eyes widened at the sight of her in her servant traveling gear. "Do you plan escaping the city? I have no guide to take us through the swamp of King Alaric's troops."

"No, Captain." She smiled at the familiarity of a companion who had faced danger with her. "This is more dangerous—the streets of Rome."

"Then it is a danger you should leave to me alone, Mistress." Manius raised a knowing eyebrow. "Stay safe. I will be your spy on the streets."

"I trust you, Captain, but I have an overwhelming need to see for myself what people are saying about Lady Serena. It's important I know how they feel."

Manius bowed. "As you will, Princess, but do you promise to obey me on the streets? Do as I say? Not draw attention to yourself?"

"I promise. I only want to listen, not to act. Where would you recommend we go?"

He rubbed his bearded jaw. "The speakers gather in the forum. There is usually a crowd outside the law courts."

"Fine. Will you escort me through the servant's quarters and out a side entrance?"

They sneaked out of the palace and made their way down the Palatine hill to the forum where people surrounded various speakers. They stopped at the edge of the first crowd, which was listening to a short man with the rounded features and good dress of a prosperous merchant.

"That Christian bitch is not only a traitor, but impious! Everyone knows how Serena snatched the necklace from Mother Goddess Rhea. The Vestal Virgin escorting the traitress was so scandalized, she cursed the unbeliever, her husband, and her children. They are all dead or dying. The curse has come to pass!"

"That heathen man is attacking Serena for being a Christian!" Placidia huffed.

Manius squeezed her arm and whispered in her ear. "Quiet, Princess. Don't rouse the mob." He maneuvered her a few feet away. "What are they talking about?"

"I was a child when Serena took the necklace from a pagan statue. Maybe twelve years ago? The curse frightened me, but Serena laughed and told me the old gods had no power, and our God would protect her from evil. I'm amazed that anyone remembers that incident. Why bring it up now?"

"Lampadius' agents will use any excuse to discredit Serena and build support for her execution." Manius frowned. "Christianity wears a thin skin in Rome. Many—perhaps the majority—still cling to the old gods."

"You're probably right. When Father outlawed all forms of paganism, Rome protested the loudest against abolishing the traditional religions. But the ruling class came around when they found Christians were favored at court. Maybe Christianity isn't as firmly rooted in the poorer classes." They turned back to listen to the tirade.

"The Pope left for Ravenna ahead of the invaders. Our 'Holy Father,' such as he is, abandoned us to the barbarians, and weathers the siege in comfort and safety!" An ominous rumbling rose from the mob. Some people trickled away from the crowd.

Fellow Christians? Placidia wondered.

"The curse on Serena will bring destruction on our city if we don't respect the old gods. They have kept us safe for hundreds of years," the merchant continued, growing red in the face from shouting. "Other cities drove off the barbarians. Do you know how they did it? With force of arms? No! They held traditional rites and asked the protection of their city gods! Their gods sent thunderstorms and lightning to harry the barbarians, and they left the cities in peace. We should do the same!"

Many shouted, "Aye, we should sacrifice to the gods!"

A mighty roar of approval drowned out any protest.

"Little good that will do!" Placidia muttered under her breath.

Manius took her arm. They drifted around the forum, from one speaker to another. The anti-barbarians were everywhere: on the speakers' platforms, under the colonnade, leading chants in the crowds. The agents appealed to the city's patriotism and pride: "No people are greater than Romans! We have conquered the world, and should not appease barbaric Goths with one bronze coin, much less gold and land!" Others slandered Stilicho as a traitor and tied Serena firmly to the invaders. The crowds coalesced into a mob crying for Serena's death like baying hounds. "Death to the traitress! Kill the bitch before she kills us!"

"There's nothing more to see here. We should go." Manius took Placidia's arm, leading the way out of the howling crowd.

Not for the first time, Placidia doubted herself. *What can I do against this mob? I'm just one voice!*

"And what of Princess Placidia?" A tall man, with gray-streaked beard and piercing blue eyes, shouted to the crowd.

Placidia stopped, forcing Manius to turn around. *What about me? Why is my name in their profane mouths?*

"What about the princess?" A confused murmur rose from the mob, echoing Placidia's thoughts.

Manius tugged her arm. She twisted away.

"Princess Placidia could rid us of Serena. Because of the siege, we cannot appeal to the emperor in Ravenna, but the princess is of imperial blood. She could condemn the traitress!"

Placidia felt a large hand cover her mouth, just as she was about to shout, "No!" She bit down, tasting blood as she struggled in Manius' grip.

"Princess, you must not say a word. Remember your promise," Manius hissed in her ear. "You must not be recognized."

"The Princess can save us!" the mob shouted. "Princess Placidia can condemn the traitress!"

She grew limp in the captain's arms, nodding.

He removed his hand from her mouth. "It's time to go home."

She nodded meekly, allowing him to lead her back to the palace in a daze. *Who are these people who want to murder an innocent woman? Will they turn on me next, if I do not do their will?*

CHAPTER 12

"You did not see them, Attalus." Placidia's hand shook at the memory of the faces haunting her nightmares: wild eyes, screaming mouths, throats in a rictus of howling. She set her goblet of wine aside to avoid sloshing its contents on her yellow silk stola. "I've never seen such hate or anger." She shuddered.

"I'm so sorry you had to go through that, Princess." Attalus set aside his own wine to take her hands in his. "You should have your captain dismissed for putting you in such danger."

At the unfair accusation, Placidia stiffened and withdrew her hands. "Manius did only what I ordered him to. The fault is entirely mine." She slumped back into her chair, nearly spitting her bitterness. "I can't say I'm glad I went into the crowds, but I did learn something important. Lampadius and his associates have a far greater grip on this city than you apparently do, Prefect."

"I-I…" His face paled. He took a deep breath, and bowed. "I'm sorry I failed you, Princess."

She waited for the excuses, the explanations. He offered none. His sincere sorrow touched her. Placidia softened. "Forgive me, Attalus. I feel helpless and take my frustration out on you. You advise me ably. I still count you a friend."

He looked her full in the face. "Hold tight those feelings of friendship. I bring you more bad tidings, Princess."

She nodded. "I probably already know, but please tell me."

"Lampadius and a delegation from the senate wish to meet with you." He hesitated.

"They want me to condemn my Aunt Serena." She sighed. "At least one of the speakers was urging that on the crowd. Lampadius can now be seen as doing the will of the Roman people. I'm sure he is pleased his agent worked so well to put me in a corner."

"He likely feels he will find an ally in you, Princess. Serena was raised in the imperial court, and is cunning in its ways. She has been skillfully using her 'former' friends to spread her own stories of the rift between you two. As far as Rome is concerned, you have broken with her family to stand by your brother. She cannot save herself, but wants to save you."

"But her family *is* my family! I don't think I can do this, Attalus." She twisted her hands in her lap. "How can I?"

"Because it is Serena's will. Find the strength."

"It's not right!" she said in a small voice.

"It is if you want to survive to fight another day." He rose and patted her shoulder. "I'll leave you now, but I'll be with the delegation tomorrow. You won't be alone."

She felt alone. Totally alone. And bereft.

"Mistress, I'm so sorry to disturb you." A scared young servant bowed, mumbling, "You have visitors."

Placidia turned over in her bed and pulled a cover over her head. "Send them away. I'm ill and wish to see no one."

She heard the girl scurry out of the room, then groaned with a headache. Not one for drinking, she had consumed more than one goblet of unwatered wine at mid-day while eating little, and now suffered the consequences. At least for an hour or two, during the afternoon, she had slept. She tried to bring back that oblivion by pulling a blanket over her head.

A fracas at the door caught her attention.

"I told you I wanted no visitors!" she screamed.

"We were told you were ill. We couldn't leave our niece alone, with only servants to care for her."

Placidia sat up as a middle-aged matron dressed in plain but expensive black silk entered the room, followed by a smaller, older woman, similarly dressed. Something about the matron looked familiar.

"Aunt Laeta?" She hadn't seen Emperor Gratian's widow since she was a little girl. Gratian, Placidia's maternal uncle, had elevated her father to co-emperor. After Gratian's death, Theodosius ruled both East and West alone and Laeta had retired to her own estates. *What is she doing here? I didn't even know she was in Rome!*

"Yes, child, and my mother Lady Tisamene."

The older woman sniffed, looking around the disheveled room. Tisamene picked a stola off the floor and returned a goblet to its upright position. "It is obvious what is ailing you, girl. Now get out of bed, get dressed, and meet us in the solar. We have business to discuss." Tisamene marched out and began ordering the servants to clean Placidia's room.

How dare she! Placidia sat up in indignation.

Laeta smiled to take the sting out of her mother's words. "She's right, Placidia. You need all your strength and wits. Wine won't help with either. We'll ask your cook to provide you with something for a sour stomach and sore head in the solar. Join us when you've cleaned up."

"At least they are family and seem concerned about me," Placidia muttered as she dragged herself from bed. "You," she ordered the nearest servant, "get Marion. I need her to dress me and fix my hair." Two other servants whisked away dirty clothes and dishes of uneaten food. A third mopped up spilled wine and remade the bed with fresh sheets.

Once she was reasonably presentable, in a plain blue linen stola with minimal gold embroidery at neck and hem, hair brushed and tamed into a neat chignon, she walked down the colonnaded hall to the solar. Overlooking a sheer cliff, the solar was her favorite room in the palace. Unlike most rooms in her suite, which only had openings on the garden, wide windows in opposite walls let in the sun and cooling breezes. She enjoyed the potted flowers that appeared in different seasons. Today was a gray, drizzly fall day, mirroring her gray and sorrowful mood. Even the lovely scent of fall roses didn't raise her spirits.

She hesitated in the doorway. Lady Tisamene sat embroidering a linen cloth, under the light of a bronze chandelier. Laeta seemed absorbed reading a slim volume of gospels. Both women appeared to subscribe to Serena's rule that idle hands indicated a lazy slothful life. Placidia agreed with the philosophy, but had always found traditional domestic tasks of spinning, weaving, sewing, and embroidery to be boring.

"Aunt Laeta, Lady Tisamene." She nodded at her distant relatives. "Have my servants taken care of your needs?"

"We're fine." Laeta indicated the light repast of stuffed eggs, cheeses, olives, crusty bread, and the always-present wine on the marble-topped sideboard. "You should eat something. Girl!" she waved at a young servant with a strawberry mark on her forearm. "Make your mistress a plate." Turning back to Placidia, Laeta patted a well-cushioned bench, "Come, child, sit at my side."

Placidia winced at the "child" designation and the implied orders in the tone of her aunt's voice. She turned to the servant. "No food or wine, but I smell ginger tisane."

The girl immediately poured a steaming cup and brought it to her. Placidia sniffed deeply of the spicy scent, then sipped it. *Honey and ginger for my stomach. And a bitter herb? Ah! Willow bark for my throbbing head.* She sometimes took a stronger dose of this mixture when her monthly courses caused her pain. She took a deep drink, then set it aside. "Thank you." She turned to Laeta and her mother. "What brings you to my home on such an inhospitable day?"

"We've come to recruit your efforts in helping the poor during this ghastly siege." Lady Tisamene set aside her embroidery to address the servants. "Leave us."

The wretched servants scattered like frightened birds. They didn't even look to Placidia for confirmation. She frowned at this additional usurpation of her authority in her own home, but held her irritation at bay. Something else was at play here. Laeta and Tisamene had not visited before, and they could certainly speak of charitable acts in front of the servants.

Laeta waited until the door whispered shut, then spoke. "Serena sent us."

"How is she? Is Tia getting better?" Placidia's hope soared for a moment, but the doleful expressions on both older women's faces told her everything she needed to know. "I would like to see my cousin before she dies. We have been great friends."

"That won't be possible, Placidia." Tisamene gave her a sharp glance. "Serena forbids you to visit or act in any way that would endanger yourself."

"I'm afraid you have a hard road ahead, child." Laeta patted her hand. "The senate demands her execution, and wants your consent. You must give it."

"But—"

"No." Laeta shook her head. "There are no 'buts.' These are dangerous times. If you do not consent, the mob will likely turn on you. Whispers come from the Ravenna court that you opposed Stilicho's execution, and are still attached to Serena."

Placidia took another sip of her ginger drink. It didn't settle her stomach. Her head started pounding. She lurched to her feet and vomited in a pot of ferns. There she stood, shaking with suppressed sobs, until she felt a warm embrace and recognized Laeta's faint lavender scent.

"I'm so sorry this burden is on your shoulders, child, but you must find the strength to endure. Your life depends on it. We've promised Serena to guide you in this."

"Tia? What will become of her?"

"I'll take in your cousin. My reputation is spotless. No one will complain about a former empress tending to a dying girl. There has been no talk of her in the forum; no threats."

Placidia shuddered again, but not from illness. She remembered the hate-filled faces in the forum. Any false courage from the wine fled. "I'll obey Serena in this. Now, please leave me."

"Of course, child." Laeta gave her a brief hug. Even Tisamene's austere face showed a hint of compassion.

The two women slipped out the door. Placidia poured herself a goblet of wine. *Serena, Attalus, and now Laeta and Tisamene; all give me the same advice. Why does such logical counsel feel so wrong?*

THE NEXT MORNING, Placidia felt no better. Head ached. Stomach roiled. Mouth tasted foul. She rolled over, tried to banish the wispy memory of nightmares. No one scene was clear, but, in the way of dreams, flashes of action melded with vivid feelings of fear and horror, leaving her with a sense of dread. Only the overwhelming needs of her body drove her from her bed, to squat over the chamber pot.

The servant who slept on the mat at the bottom of her bed jumped up to attend her.

"Go away," Placidia mumbled.

The girl turned sorrowful eyes on her, and backed toward the door.

"Wait!" Placidia ran a hand through her tangled curls. "I need a bath. Tell the bath attendants, and send in Marion."

The girl curtsied and skittered out the door. Immediately after, Marion—the middle-aged woman who dressed her and arranged her hair—came in, bearing a tray of crisp brown rolls with melted cheese, ripe purple grapes, sliced apples, and the familiar-smelling ginger tisane with willow bark. Of course, Paulus knew of her overindulgence, and had planned for the aftermath. The old soldier had lots of personal experience to draw on.

Placidia's stomach rebelled at the scents, but she kept her bile down. While Marion combed out her hair, she nibbled on a roll and gulped the ginger drink. Again, she took a deep breath, swallowing the bile that rose in her throat. *So, this is the horrible feeling soldiers complain about after a night in the taverns. Why do they go back to repeat it, time after time?*

As Aunt Laeta had warned, wine did not solve her problems, only added to them. Placidia vowed never to repeat her own sorry performance. *Enough! It's time to start acting like the daughter of the Great Theodosius and do my duty.*

With that reminder, she straightened her shoulders, lifted her head, and inspected the image in her polished silver mirror. Youth masked much of the damage. Her eyes were slightly reddened, and shadows darkened the skin underneath. *Nothing an eye wash and bit of face powder can't disguise.*

After a hot soak in her private bath, Placidia reclined on the massage table, groaning as the sloe-eyed Greek slave worked her magic on the knots and kinks in her back and shoulders. While the slave scraped the oil off her body, Marion entered the room. "Princess, a message from Prefect Attalus." She winced at Placidia's frown. "The messenger said it was urgent."

"Of course." Placidia sat up and held out her hand for the missive. She skimmed the brief note, then nodded. "Tell the messenger to tell the Prefect, I will be ready." The dresser turned to leave. "And Marion…" The woman turned back with a carefully blank face. "…meet me in my rooms after. I must prepare for a delegation from the senate."

The woman bowed and left.

Now it begins. Or ends.

CHAPTER 13

Marion piled Placidia's hair in the current style of complicated braids and false curls. "Drape the rope of pearls around my hair, Marion. I want it to mimic an imperial diadem." *It will be a long time before I can wear a true one. I doubt Honorius will elevate me to Augusta anytime soon.*

Marion dressed her with care in an imperial purple silk stola heavily embroidered with gold and pearls at the neck, sleeve, and hem. Underneath, she wore a vivid yellow linen tunica. She didn't care for purple, it made her skin look sallow, but she needed to project an imperial presence.

When the dresser reached for her cosmetics, Placidia stayed her hand. "A light touch for today. Only ointment and powder, to cover the darkness under the eyes, and a narrow line of kohl. I want to look older than my years, but not haggard."

Marion nodded and did as she asked. Placidia was pleased with the image in the mirror. She might not be traditionally beautiful, but her expressive brown eyes made up for those minor flaws. Her face and figure should be eclipsed by her imperial bearing. *The Senators will not see me as a cowed young girl, but a strong woman—a Theodosian woman—a woman of authority. I need to act like Serena and, if possible, forestall my aunt's doom.*

The reminder of the purpose of the meeting brought a lump to her throat and tightness to her chest. She suppressed her tears with grim determination. She dared not look weak, even in front of her servants. Placidia steeled her face.

"Bring me my jewel box."

Marion lugged over a heavy cedar box, decorated with a leaf and flower pattern picked out in gold and inlaid with mother-of-pearl. Placidia opened the lid to rummage through the silk sacks holding gold and silver rings, bracelets, and chains of amethysts, amber, and pearls—a meager selection of her favorite pieces from Ravenna. Honorious had kept the rest. She pushed gold bracelets onto her wrists and looped a double chain of purple amethysts around her neck.

"Perfect." Placidia smiled. "Tell Manius to attend me in the receiving room, and send Paulus in."

"Yes, Mistress." Marion left.

Placidia moved to her outer chamber and sat, breathing shallowly, preparing for the ordeal to come. Not just meeting the senators, but telling Paulus what she planned to do. How would Stilicho's most loyal servant react when she told him she might be forced to condemn Stilicho's wife?

She twitched when the outer door opened. The old soldier limped in on his crutch.

"Princess, you wished to see me?"

"Please sit, Paulus. There is no need for ceremony between us." She pointed to a chair.

Paulus folded his spare frame onto the cushioned seat, looking at her expectantly.

"Have you heard the rumors in the city about Lady Serena?" she asked.

"Lies!" he snorted. "My mistress would never betray her city or the empire."

"Of course not! It is the same faction in Rome that caused Stilicho's death in Ravenna. They are using the siege to finish wiping out Stilicho's family. Serena and I are the last relatives who might have some influence over my half-witted brother."

"Do we return to Ravenna?"

"No. It is too late for that." Placidia shook her head. "I cannot leave during the siege. I would be too valuable a hostage." She hesitated, gathering her wits. "I face a horrible choice, Paulus. Lampadius and the anti-barbarians have roused the city against Serena. They will come here soon to ask for my permission to execute her."

Paulus' face darkened. "You won't consent." The angry words were a statement, not a question.

"Serena advises me to."

"No." The old man's face twisted into a hurt scowl.

"With her family dead and dying, she no longer wishes to live. She believes that, by playing this part, I can survive and fight another day." Placidia's voice cracked with tears. "I don't want to do it, Paulus, but I'm afraid. I could lose my life, as well. Serena, Attalus, even Aunt Laeta tell me to consent. What should I do?"

The blood drained from Paulus' face. His mouth opened but no words came out.

A wave of revulsion crested in Placidia's soul. *How could I be so weak? Begging this faithful servant to approve my heinous act, making him complicit in his former mistress' death?*

"No. Don't answer me." She rose and strode over to the old man slumped in the soft chair. "It is unfair to ask. This is my decision, and mine alone." She patted his trembling shoulder.

"What will you do, Princess?" He looked up with anguished eyes.

"I don't know." She dragged reluctant feet to the door of the outer room, then turned back. "You should not greet the senators, or be within their sight. I don't want you hauled out of the palace as a possible spy."

The suggestion put steel back in the old soldier's spine. He stood. "You are my mistress now. I am loyal to you, and you alone. Whatever you decide. I swear—" He put his hand where his sword once hung, then covered his heart instead. "—to give my life for yours, to obey you in all things, or spend eternity in a fiery pit."

"Thank you, Paulus." His devotion brought another wave of doubt. If she fell to the mob, what would become of her household? "I pray that won't be required of you today."

PLACIDIA PROCEEDED DOWN THE COLONNADED WALKWAY toward her private receiving room. This wasn't the lavish hall that emperors used to hold court in the palace, but it was large and impressive, clad in marble of all colors. Niches held sculptures, copies of Greek classics, painted in vivid colors and decorated in gold and bronze. At the far end, a low dais held a gilded chair padded with purple cushions. Ebony tables stood conspicuously unadorned by food or drink behind the mini throne. There were no benches or chairs for visitors. Manius stood by, looking formidable in full armor and livery.

She smiled. All was as she ordered.

Placidia approached the gilded chair, lowered herself onto the cushions, and waved Manius over. "Have my visitors arrived?"

"A few moments ago, Princess."

"Let them wait a quarter hour, then bring them in."

"As you command." He bowed briefly, then left the room.

Placidia sat brooding. Her mind tossed out one improbable action after another, twisting like a hare caught in a trap. A wave of thirst dried her mouth. She regretted not having water in the room.

A servant appeared at her elbow and said, in a muffled voice, "Your guests are coming, Princess."

"Bring me a goblet of water, then go."

He bowed out, returning almost immediately with a pitcher of water, condensation beading on the smooth silver sides of the beaker. He poured water into a ruby red glass goblet chased with a silver rim and stem, then left the goblet on a small table set to the left of her chair.

She downed the water in a couple of gulps, just before Manius arrived at the door to announce her guests. "Prefect Priscus Attalus, Senator Lampadius, and a further delegation of five Conscript Fathers…" Manius proceeded to name five of the most prominent men in Rome. "…to petition Your Nobilissima."

Placidia suppressed a smile at the slight frown on Lampadius' face when he surveyed the formal room, and his wince when Manius used the word "petition." The senator shot Attalus a calculating look. *Thought you would surprise me in an informal situation, Senator? Hoped to dominate me with the number and importance of your male entourage? Have you never dealt with a Theodosian?* This small victory gave Placidia a dash of confidence.

Lampadius smoothed his face and stilled his body. No one could speak or approach until she allowed it. She waited, studying every man in the delegation as if weighing his worth. When a couple of them started shuffling their feet, she finally spoke. "You may approach and present your petition."

Manius escorted the delegation to the foot of Placidia's dais, then took his place at her right, his hand on the hilt of his sword. The senators bowed low. She didn't expect a full obeisance—that was reserved for those holding the title of Augustus or Augusta—but was pleased with the courtesy shown her. Attalus stood slightly apart from the group, offering her a small smile as he rose from his bow.

Lampadius stepped forward. "Our Most Wise and Gracious Princess, we come to you today for help with a grave threat to the security of our city." He turned to indicate the other five senators. "We are the most senior Conscript Fathers, tasked with the charge of representing and protecting the people of Rome. It has come to our attention that there is a spy in our midst."

"I suspect there are many spies in the city. We hold many Goths, Suevis, and other barbarians as slaves. It is to be expected that they would favor their own tribe. What is your plan to deal with them?" Placidia thought to distract Lampadius from his mission, but failed.

"As our wise Prefect recommended, they are to be expelled from the city, to burden Alaric and his rabble." Lampadius waved his hand dismissively. "I speak of the wife of that traitor Stilicho."

"You speak of Lady Serena, my cousin, adopted sister, and the woman who raised me."

Attalus frowned, giving a slight shake of his head.

"We have evidence from a household slave that Serena plots with that so-called 'King of the Goths' to betray our city."

Placidia leaned back in her chair. This was a new and damning accusation. "Evidence obtained by torture; I assume?" That was the traditional way of gaining evidence from slaves.

He nodded. "Of course, Princess."

"Corroborated by any citizen?"

"No, but the story of Serena's perfidy has circulated in the population, and the people of Rome demand her death." Lampadius spoke with conviction. "We cannot ignore her crimes and the judgement of the people. She must be executed."

"Then go to my brother and demand justice. Only the Augustus can condemn another member of the imperial family."

"We cannot get through the siege. You represent your brother here in Rome." Lampadius indicated the formal receiving room, looking pointedly at her imperial attire. "You must condemn Serena."

Placidia stiffened, inwardly groaning. She had hoped the imperial trappings would give her more influence, allow her to cow her opponents. Instead, Lampadius used them to justify his demands of her. She represented the Imperial Authority in Rome, and was neatly caught.

Taking advantage of her hesitation, Lampadius put on a sorrowful face. He extended his hands palms up, as if showing his helplessness. "The people are frightened and angry, Princess. They are on the verge of plucking the traitress from her home and exacting justice themselves on Serena and all her household. After that, who knows what they would do?" He shrugged.

And there it is: the threat behind the request. If I do not give in, Tia might die, and he will turn the people of Rome against me.

"You are asking me to do an unnatural thing: condemn a member of the imperial family to death," she said quietly.

"A woman who would betray her city and people. Those same people are on the verge of rioting. That would be disastrous for our city. A city divided cannot stand against invaders. You must condemn Serena, to save your people." He held out a short sheet of parchment.

Manius stepped forward, took the missive, and handed it to Placidia. She read the brief declaration:

> *It is resolved by both the whole Senate in common with and by Galla Placidia Noblissima, sister of the emperor by the same father, that Serena, wife of the traitor Stilicho, be put to death, being the cause of the evils hemming them in: the siege of Rome by Alaric and his army.*

"Prefect, do you concur?" She looked desperately at Attalus. There had to be another way!

"I do, Princess."

She shook her head. The parchment fluttered from nerveless fingers. "I need time. This is a terrible thing you ask of me. Come back next week."

Lampadius swooped in for the kill. "We have no time, Princess!" he boomed. "The people are in the streets as we speak. Give your consent to the death of one traitor now, or be responsible for hundreds or thousands of innocent lives later."

Attalus picked up the death warrant and returned it to her hands, murmuring, "It is Serena's wish. Take control of your fate." He stepped back.

She read the hateful declaration again, stood, and handed it back to Lampadius. "You have my consent. You are all witnesses." *And I won't forget your part in this.* She again inspected each man's face, committing them to memory. "Now leave my presence."

The senators beat a hasty retreat.

Attalus stayed for moment to say, "You did the right thing, Princess."

"Did I?" she whispered to herself. She let tears streak her face as the Prefect left her chamber.

"Princess?" Manius looked overwhelmed by her emotion.

"I wish to be left alone."

"As you command." The captain backed out of the room, relief warring with concern on his face.

CHAPTER 14

The next day, Paulus limped into her receiving room, tears streaming down his face. "It's done, Mistress. Attalus sent word that Lady Serena has been strangled in the forum. The crowds cheered. God curse them!"

"Leave me, Paulus." She looked around at the myriad faces of her servants: some grieving, some shocked, a few perfectly neutral. "Out! All of you." They left. Placidia took to her bed. *Stilicho, Eucherius, Serena, and soon Tia. Why have I survived?* The world lost all color as she pushed her emotions into a small dark corner of her soul, holding them there lest they flood her body with pain and guilt. She didn't cry or sob.

Over the next few days, Placidia refused to talk to Paulus or see Attalus. Food and wine had no taste. She left tantalizing dishes untouched. Fresh flowers smelled of death; music sounded dull and mournful, no matter how lively the tune. She sat in the dark, suspended between disgust and guilt and sadness.

On the fifth day, she heard a commotion at her sitting room door, but ignored it, returning to her dreary nothingness.

"Placidia!" A quiet but commanding voice echoed in her ears. "Child, it is time to put grieving aside and take your place in the world."

Aunt Laeta? Placidia mumbled, "Go away."

"At least it's not wine, this time," an older, more querulous voice added from a corner. "Thank the Good Lord for small blessings."

"Mother! Can't you see the child is distraught."

"She's no longer a child." Lady Tisamene's voice sounded closer. "She's taken on imperial responsibilities and needs to learn how to live with that. Placidia!" Tisamene turned Placidia's face to hers, raised her hand, and slapped her.

Placidia yelped, putting her hand against her stinging face. *How dare she!* Outrage at the physical assault burned away the fog. She looked around the room. The women's faces came into focus.

Tisamene grabbed Placidia's shoulders and shook her. "Serena did not sacrifice her life so you could waste yours cowering in the dark. Show some spine, girl!"

"Enough!" Placidia groaned.

Tisamene stared into her eyes. "Good. She's got some sense back." The old woman moved to the windows and pushed the shutters open, letting in the late morning sun and a cool fall breeze. "It stinks in here. When was the last time you bathed?"

A hot blush crept up Placidia's neck and face. "I-I don't know."

"She speaks!" Tisamene declared with dripping sarcasm.

"Mother, please! Get Placidia food and drink. Leave us to talk."

"Talk never did anyone any good." Tisamene turned to the door. "Action, Daughter! Action! If you dwell too much in the mind, you lose yourself." The door banged shut behind her.

Laeta sighed. "She does have a point, child, even if she is harsh in stating it. You do yourself and your people little good, hiding in a dark room. The siege goes on. The people grow more desperate. You are the daughter of the Great Theodosius, and sister to the emperor. The people of Rome look to you for guidance and succor. It is time to put away your grief and tend to them." Laeta sat beside Placidia, taking her in her arms.

"It's not grief; it's guilt." Placidia gulped. "I gave my consent to Serena's execution." Tears flowed easily down her cheeks. Her chest tightened with sobs. Placidia turned to the comforting form of her distant aunt and let out the torrent of weeping she had suppressed for days. She had missed the comfort of an older woman's guidance.

The physical release triggered an emotional one, as well. "It hurts!" she gasped.

"I know, child, I've lived through many a loss." Laeta patted her back. "Trust me, hoarding pain and feeding guilt makes them stronger. Face your loss. Pain dulls and fades with time. Forgive yourself. You did what was necessary. It's time to acknowledge that. You cannot change the past, but you control what you do in the present. What would Serena want of you? You are her only legacy now."

"I tried to be the woman she was and…and…I failed," Placidia mumbled into Laeta's ample bosom. "That awful Lampadius turned my imperial pretensions against me."

"Pretensions? That's part of the problem. You aren't playing a part, or asking for power. You are an imperial princess, and have power. But imperial women must learn to wield that power differently than imperial men. We don't command armies, write laws, or judge people as magistrates, but we can win the affection and loyalty of the men who do."

"Hah!" Tisamene's derisive snort startled Placidia. She hadn't heard the older woman return. "Put the platter over there and leave us."

The servants deposited a platter with the tantalizing smells of fresh baked bread, smoked fish, and sharp cheese wafting from it. Placidia's stomach rumbled in response. She broke from Laeta's clasp.

"Thank you, Lady Tisamene." Placidia covered a warm roll with cheese and wolfed it down. That morsel satisfied her stomach. She poured herself a goblet of water freshened with mint.

"So, she lives, after all!" Tisamene chortled. "But don't believe all that nonsense my daughter is feeding you about exercising imperial power through men. That only works when you are young and beautiful, because men think with their mentulae."

"Mother!" Laeta blushed at the use of the common word for a male member.

"Placidia has grown up around soldiers. I'm sure she's heard worse words."

"Humph. That doesn't mean you have to say them." Laeta crossed her arms over her chest in disapproval.

Placidia smiled at the small disagreement between mother and daughter.

"Where was I?" Tisamene sucked her teeth in concentration. "Yes! In Laeta's world, when your youth and beauty fades, your power fades. Money is also a two-edged sword. If men do what you want for money alone, someone else can buy them for more. You can never be sure of their loyalty. Power lies with the people."

"What?" Placidia gaped.

"How did Lampadius defeat you? Did he threaten you personally? Did he trick you into your consent? No. He roused the mob. He had the people of Rome behind him."

Placidia shuddered at the memories of screaming people in the forum. "But they are so dangerous and unpredictable."

"Not with leaders of strong character and deep moral fiber. It is your duty as a Theodosian and imperial princess to lead and care for your people. Be decisive. Act. Do God's work among the poor, and they will follow and love you. Anyone with the people of Rome behind them is a formidable force. It is time you went out among the people and let them know you."

Tisamene softened her tone. "It's not just for duty or power. Work soothes the mind. God's work soothes the soul. God and the people will judge you by your actions, not your words. Come, Daughter." Tisamene snapped her fingers at Laeta. "Let's leave Placidia to pray and contemplate our advice."

"Be well, child. Take the day to calm yourself. We'll be back tomorrow." Laeta gave a final pat to Placidia's hand before standing.

"Be ready at the second hour." Tisamene offered a faint smile. "We will collect you to join our mission to distribute food to the poor. This siege is only days old, but the poorest are suffering already as prices in the market soar. I have faith that you will acquit yourself well."

After the ladies left, Placidia took stock of herself. She couldn't change the past, but she could learn from it. Stilicho and Serena were no longer able to give her advice, but she could learn from their examples of duty and service: to family, to the people, to the empire. Laeta and Tisamene were also right. There were many ways to access and wield power. If she wanted to protect herself and the ones she loved, she needed to learn to do better. She needed to bring all her resources to bear.

Placidia sniffed her stale odor, wrinkled her nose, and said to herself, "But first a bath."

CHAPTER 15

Placidia returned from her fifth charity mission in five days to find Attalus waiting in her work room. "Prefect! To what do I owe this visit?"

"I heard you were among the living again, and came to see for myself." His smile took the sting out of his words. "It seems Lady Laeta and Lady Tisamene had the desired effect."

"You sent them?" Placidia briefly wavered between annoyance at the Prefect's meddling and gratitude for his solicitous affection. Gratitude won out.

"I let them know your condition, yes, but they chose to come. May I?" He pointed to a pitcher of wine on the sideboard.

She nodded. "I'm sure it's a good vintage. My servants know your preferences."

He smiled, poured for both, and brought over a goblet for her. "I hope you've forgiven me, Princess."

"For gossiping to Aunt Laeta and Lady Tisamene?" Placidia sat in an ebony chair, sighing. She was tired after being on her feet for hours, passing out bread and apples to poor families who couldn't afford market prices. It was a pleasant tiredness, suffused with the satisfaction of a good deed well done.

Attalus shook his head, "No. For my part in Lady Serena's death."

"I forgive you, Attalus." *Even if I can't forgive myself.* Her mouth twisted into a bitter smile. "Lampadius both failed and succeeded. The Goths didn't turn tail at the news of Serena's execution, but there is one less Theodosian to influence my brother." Placidia took a sip of her wine, then gave the prefect a sharp look. "What news from the senate's meeting with Alaric? I assume you attended?"

"I was there, and the news is not good. Lampadius and his delegation offered the original four thousand pounds of gold agreed to by Stilicho for the Goths to retreat."

Placidia snorted. "After defaming my uncle for offering the same deal, he could do no better?"

"Even worse." Attalus took a gulp of the wine. "Alaric replied he would take all the gold, silver, jewels, furniture, and other valuables of the citizens of the city. When Lampadius cried that would leave them nothing, Alaric laughed and said, 'I leave you your lives.'"

"Did the delegation counter? The senators' wealth comes from their land. They can afford to give up some extra silver, gold, and jewels to save the people from a ruinous siege." From the rueful expression on Attalus' face, she guessed the response. "Those selfish, vain fools! They didn't even try to negotiate?"

"They were outraged, and broke off the talks."

"Alaric will block our grain from Africa and seize all the resources of the hinterlands." She set her goblet aside, chewing her lip as she did rapid calculations. "I've seen the granaries and warehouses. With the food we moved into the city, we cannot feed hundreds of thousands of people for more than a month, even on half rations."

"One good thing came out of the negotiations. Alaric has agreed to let us send a delegation to Ravenna to petition Pope Innocent."

"Petition the Pope for what? A miracle?"

"No." Attalus laughed. "Ostensibly for the Pope's return to the city, but, in reality, they want his permission to hold pagan rites to drive off the Goths. Many Romans still believe in the old gods and feel it's the fault of the weak Christian God that we're suffering."

"Before the siege, I saw a man haranguing the mob with stories about other cities driving off the Goths with the help of their city deities. I had no idea the pagans had so much influence with the Senate."

"I'm afraid, Princess, that many in Rome don't believe in the Christian God." The smile fled his face. "Including me."

"You're a pagan?" Placidia gasped.

"A philosopher. There's a difference. I believe in one supreme creative force— call it God, if you will. The world is full of gods, prophets, magicians, and miracle workers; one little different than the next. Christ is only the most recent to grab the imagination of the masses." He studied her face. "I hope I haven't shocked you, Princess."

Placidia shook her head. "Not shocked. Surprised at your honesty. Ravenna is packed with people who flocked to the baptismal fonts to get ahead at a Christian court. If they have doubts, they keep them to themselves. You risk much by not following in their footsteps."

"I know." Attalus shrugged. "Our delegation will be disappointed. The Bishop of Rome will stay safe in Ravenna and will never sanction pagan rites. However, the effort provides me with an opportunity. One of the members will be my envoy. He will meet with the emperor, tell him of our dire fate, and ask for help. Honorius refused us before, but surely he will come to Rome's rescue now."

"I'm not so sure." Placidia shook her head. "My brother decimated his army when he expelled the barbarians. I don't know what troops he has available or whether he would spare them for us." She thought a moment. "I don't know how much help it will be, but I can add my voice to yours. I'd like to send my captain to Ravenna with a letter to Honorius."

"Manius? He's a fine soldier. Can you spare him?"

"I'm less in need of protection, now that Serena's gone. I've been among the poor and witnessed their suffering. They are no threat to me. Are you aware of any plots against me among the aristocracy?"

"No, Princess. Your good works are already being emulated by other prominent ladies. Everyone speaks of your nobility in both ridding the city of a traitor and doing God's work among the poor."

Placidia winced at the reference to her collusion with the senate in her aunt's death. *That betrayal will forever stain my soul. But Lady Tisamene had been right; work soothed the mind, and God's work soothed the soul—a double advantage.* "When is the delegation leaving?"

"Tomorrow, from the Salarian Gate, at the second hour."

"Manius will be there with my message." Placidia stood, signaling the end of the interview. "Thank you for the news, Prefect. I wish to be included in any future planning by the city fathers."

"Of course, Princess." Attalus stiffly bowed over her hand, then backed out the door, a slight frown marking his handsome face.

Why is he upset? Was he perturbed by me wanting to be included in planning? If Lampadius and the senate want my imperial authority to back them up, they will have to deal with my wishes. Attalus should know that. He had always taken a protective stance toward her. Perhaps he was saddened by her loss of political innocence—a necessary and inevitable effect of growing up and taking responsibility for her imperial presence. She shook her head. *Whatever the cause, we will work things out, my friend. Now, I have a letter to write.*

Placidia shook off her reverie, went to her desk, and pulled out a sheet of stiff parchment. She struggled with the words, wadding up several draft attempts in frustration. Finally, after an hour, she sanded a page, setting the ink:

Dearest Brother and most Honored Augustus,

Greetings from your loving sister. I know you are angry with me for leaving the court without your permission. I didn't leave because I lack love for you, Brother. I left because I had so much love for our cousin Tia. She was ill and needed me more than you did. Please take pity on two young girls who love each other as sisters, and forgive me.

Even if you cannot yet forgive me, I beg you to not abandon your loyal citizens in Rome. The siege is heavy, and the city is in dire straits. Your subjects need an army to drive off Alaric, followed by immediate shipments of food and medicine. They look to their ever-benevolent Augustus to care for them in this terrible time. I praise your name everyday among the poor and tell them how their Augustus is their Father and will not forget them.

For the love of God, and in Christian charity, see to the safety and well-being of your suffering subjects.

With sincerest wishes for your excellent health and daily prayers for your long reign, your loving sister, by her own hand,

Galla Placidia Nobilissima
Imperial Palace
Rome

Placidia folded the missive, dripped hot wax on it, and sealed it with her signet ring. Perhaps this letter could convince her brother to act with some sense. She prayed it would, but held little hope in her heart.

"YOU WISHED TO SEE ME, PRINCESS?" Manius stood at ease in her office doorway, dressed in imperial livery.

"Yes, Captain. I have a final mission for you."

His face paled at the word 'final,' but he entered her chamber, bowing slightly. "As you command, Princess. What is my mission?"

She handed over the sealed letter addressed to her brother. "Alaric is allowing a delegation from the religious community to leave the city and go to Ravenna to petition the Pope. I wish you to accompany them as part of their guard, and deliver this letter to the emperor. Prefect Attalus will also send a delegate to petition my brother for military relief. You will present my letter with his."

"If the prefect has a delegate, why not send your letter with him? Or send another? Surely, I'm more valuable to you here. The siege grows worse. There might be threats to your person. If the barbarians breach the walls, I can fight."

"Please sit, Captain." She indicated a backless camp chair. "I've thought about this thoroughly. You have served my family most loyally: Stilicho, Tia, and me. I wish to reward you, while I can. You are right that the siege grows more intense, and the senate's ineptness in managing the negotiation will only make things worse. Depending on how long the siege lasts, all households will be affected, even the imperial one."

"But—"

She raised a hand to stop his protest. "Take this, Captain." She handed him another letter with her seal but no address. "This is a recommendation from me should you wish to join a private citizen's guards. I doubt you would be welcomed in the Imperial Guard of Scholae in Ravenna, and my recommendation will have little or no weight there, but if you have some patron at the court...?"

"No, Princess, I have no patron in Ravenna." Manius shook his head with a rueful smile. "I burned those bridges when I arranged for you and the Augusta to leave."

"But you do have a friend at the palace. The cook, Marta. Angelus' cousin?"

A most becoming blush stained the captain's face. "How did—?"

"Angelus told me, while we waited for that blasted wagon to be pulled out of the mud the last time. When you get to Ravenna, would you check on the boy? His grandmother was sick. If he needs anything, can I count on you to handle it?" Placidia smiled at the memory of the precocious young swamp rat. He seemed the type that could take care of himself, but life as a peasant could be precarious. An adult male and a little extra coin could make a substantial difference in a poor child's life.

"Of course, Princess."

"This should help." Placidia handed Manius a heavy, clinking bag. "If you decide not to go into someone else's guards, this should be enough for you to buy a shop or a farm, get married, and start a family."

"Princess, you are too generous!" He stood to bow over her hand.

"Nonsense! Loyalty such as yours deserves reward. Besides—" She smiled. "—you eat too much. By sending you off to Ravenna, we will have more food for the rest of the household."

Her joke fell flat. He sobered at the reminder of the dire situation she would face without him and started to hand the money back.

"No, Captain." She withdrew her hands and stated, in a stern voice, "This is my command. Leave Rome. Deliver my message to the emperor. Live a full and happy life. Care for Marta and our little Angelus."

He saluted Placidia. "As you command, Princess." His voice did not waver, but Placidia thought she caught a hint of moisture in his dark eyes as he continued, "And may God bless and keep you safe."

When Manius left, she dashed tears from her own eyes. Another person she cared for leaving her. At least she had provided means for his survival and happiness.

This was a good act. Now, how to provide for the rest of my household, and my city?

Chapter 16

In early December, Placidia reviewed the household stores with Paulus. He carefully ticked off the list on his waxed tablet. "We have only two measures of grain, a sack of beans, and a handful of dried roots. The garden is completely bare, and we have no fruits or greens. We've been on half rations for a month, and this will not last us the week." He carefully locked the pantry and handed her the key. "Is there nothing we can buy in the market?"

"God blast the hoarders!" Placidia shook her head. "Not at any price. Our charitable ladies have bought all there is, and the churches have distributed the last of the bread. The horses, dogs and cats are gone. Even the rats are getting scarce. If the senate does not negotiate soon, Alaric can walk through gates guarded by starved corpses."

The death toll had risen steadily. At first it was the old and infirm. She lost an elderly scribe in the first wave. Then, children started to succumb. A steady procession of small coffins clogged the streets next to the emptying warehouses where the bodies were stored until they could be buried outside the city walls. The problem only worsened as various plagues and fevers broke out all over the city. There were rumors of cannibalism.

No household was immune. Placidia, Laeta, Tisamene and the other ladies switched from providing food to setting up hospitals and providing nursing services. Even that work dwindled as people were too weak to move their sick ones from home.

"How is Marion faring?" Placidia's personal body servant was the most recent victim in her household. She had come down with a fever a week ago, but seemed on the road to recovery.

"Marion died last night."

Placidia rounded on the old man but couldn't summon the energy to be angry. "When were you going to tell me?"

He looked puzzled. "I didn't intend to keep it from you. I just forgot."

She saw his hands trembling. "Of course, Paulus. We're all more forgetful these days. Our minds cannot hold anything when our bellies are empty."

"There was something else…" Paulus squinted as if trying to see something far away. A smile brightened his face. "Yes! Attalus sent word. He will be by for a visit this afternoon."

"Good. I need to talk to him."

When Attalus arrived, he cut short her protestations about hospitality, instead looking her up and down. "You're too thin! The sister of the emperor should not be in distress."

"When poor children starve in the streets, it is unseemly I and mine should sleep with full bellies."

"The poor starve in the street, whether there are barbarians at the gates or not," he said gently. He unwrapped a large, awkward bundle. "I've brought you a cheese."

Placidia's mouth watered at the nutty smell of the yellow lump. It would feed her household for days. "Where did you get it?"

"As prefect, I have a few sources not available to others. If you need anything at all, send me word." She noted that he seemed a little thinner, and gray streaked his hair, but he exuded more energy than anyone else she knew.

"Thank you, Attalus. You have been a good friend."

"I'm serious, Placidia. Do not starve yourself. Your people need you."

She sighed. "I have nothing more to give to my people."

"Your presence gives them hope," he pleaded. "Besides, don't you want to be a thorn in Lampadius' side? He would be delighted to have your voice silenced. More senators heed your common-sense suggestions than follow his fanatic bluster these days."

She smiled at the thought. "Then slice me a piece of this cheese and let's conspire to ruin Lampadius' day."

*****

ONE MID-DECEMBER MORNING, Placidia sat quietly at her desk, sipping a cup of well-watered wine, her mind blank. A nagging feeling roused her. *What's happening to me? My thoughts keep slipping away.* Placidia looked around the empty room. The servants were gone; sick or dead. The contributions from Attalus had slowed to a tiny trickle. *So, this is what it's like to starve. I don't even feel hungry. I must act or we won't survive.*

She looked down at the note she had started writing to her Aunt Laeta and Lady Tisamene. She was to meet with the senators again this afternoon, to try to persuade them to negotiate further with Alaric, and needed their presence. *Damn the senate for their obstinacy!*

She completed her plea for her older relatives to join her for the meeting. Miraculously, or because of Laeta's tender care, Tia still lived, but was too ill to leave her bed. Placidia put down her pen to wipe away a tear. *Tia, I so wish you could be at my side! We need a solid front of imperial ladies if we're to knock sense into these stubborn old men.*

She shook her head. *No time for dreaming. Back to work.*

THIS TIME, WHEN PAULUS ANNOUNCED THE SENATE DELEGATION, Placidia wore only her purple stola as a sign of her rank, her hair in a simple chignon. Laeta and Tisamene sat in less ornate chairs to her left and right, dressed in their usual somber black. None wore jewelry, or any other sign of wealth, besides their signet rings. Placidia watched Lampadius carefully as the delegation assembled at the dais to offer the imperial women a deep bow. She kept her face impassive even when Attalus gave her a brief smile and raised eyebrow. The prefect would see soon enough what she had in mind.

"Conscript Fathers, how go negotiations with the Goths?" Placidia stabbed Lampadius with a sharp stare.

The delegation exchanged looks of consternation. Lampadius—thinner, but still stocky—stepped forward. "Princess, Ladies." He nodded to Laeta and Tisamene. "We have not resumed negotiations with the barbarians. Their demands are impossible."

Placidia raised an eyebrow. "Gold, silver, jewels are just things, Senator, and easily replaced. I've spent my own fortune providing for the poor in this city, as have these ladies. Lives are being lost every day to starvation and sickness.

90

People cannot be replaced."

"If we go back to the Goths now, we speak from a position of weakness, Princess." Lampadius gave her a condescending smile.

"If we wait until the people of Rome are dead, does that strengthen our position?" Placidia snapped.

"Princess," he soothed, "we still hold out hope that your brother, our Esteemed Emperor, will send troops to lift the s—"

"That hope is in vain, Senator!" Placidia interrupted. "He will send no troops. We must make our own fate."

"Do you have information not available to us, Princess?"

"As you and your esteemed colleagues know—" she gave them a chilly smile "—I represent the emperor in Rome. In his name, I have gone among our citizens. I have ministered to their needs with the help of these good ladies and more, including your own wife, Lampadius. Has she not told you who the people hold responsible for their wretched condition?"

"My gracious lady wife has told me of some whispering among the rabble."

"The whispers grow stronger, Senators. They are becoming shouts. The names most on their lips are yours."

"But, Princess, we are not resp—"

"I want this siege lifted." Placidia rose, pointing at Lampadius. "The people of Rome want this siege lifted. Go! Negotiate a settlement as if your life depended on it." She left the threat hanging.

Lampadius took an involuntary step back. The other men stood in stunned silence.

Attalus stepped forward. "Yes, Gracious Princess. It is more than time. I will lead the delegation myself."

"Thank you, Prefect." She nodded. "I and the people of Rome will be in your debt." She turned to face the remaining delegation. "Report back to me upon your successful conclusion."

They backed toward the door, murmuring well-wishes for her life and health.

After they cleared the room, Placidia collapsed onto her chair with a gusty sigh. "That's done, then. I hope I did right."

"It was well done, Placidia." Laeta patted her hand.

"You are a worthy off-spring of your noble father." Tisamene smiled. "You managed those lumps of useless horseshit like a true Theodosian."

Laeta winced at her mother's vulgarity.

Placidia smiled, a warm glow replacing the hollow emptiness in her stomach and her heart.

PLACIDIA SPOONED THIN GRUEL INTO PAULUS' MOUTH. "You must regain your strength, old man. It is the day of our Savior's birth, and our prayers are answered. The siege is lifted. We will soon have food enough for all."

Paulus' eyes turned vaguely toward her voice. "Alaric, gone?"

"The gates are open. Alaric allows a market and people rejoice in the streets."

"At what price?"

Placidia was puzzled at first by the question, then realized Paulus wanted to know how much Rome had to pay to be rid of the barbarians.

"Only a little less than what Alaric demanded. We emptied the mint, stripped the buildings and statues, and melted our artwork and jewelry to make the price—five thousand pounds of gold and thirty thousand of silver. And just to puncture the vanity of the stiff-necked Romans, Alaric insisted on our stores of red leather, silk, and pepper. The senators of Rome will have to do without their red boots this season, and their ladies without silken stolas."

Paulus let out a soft sigh, closing his eyes. Placidia's heart skipped a beat. She held the spoon in a death grip until Paulus' chest rose and fell with a shallow breath. The spoon clattered to the floor. She huddled in her chair for a moment, in relief. *Not today!*

Weeks of grief and privation had dried her tears. She considered the row of bodies in the cold cellar, wrapped in linen, awaiting burial beyond the gates. "You won't be joining them, Paulus." She tenderly pushed a lock of gray hair off his forehead.

And to think, this waste could have been avoided with a little enlightened diplomacy on my brother's part. If I ruled...

Placidia sighed, set the bowl of gruel on the side table, and pulled a woolen blanket over the old soldier's frail frame.

If I ruled...

She went to her workroom to write another letter to her brother. As part of the Gothic king's demands, the prefect and a delegation ventured to Ravenna tomorrow to implore the emperor to make a permanent peace with Alaric. Attalus had asked her to lend her voice to their appeals. *As if it will do any better*

92

than my last letter. Placidia dipped her pen in the ink and wrote,

Dearest Brother and most Honored Augustus,

Greetings from your loving sister. You have chosen not to respond to my earlier appeals, but I beg you again not to abandon the loyal citizens of Rome. The siege is lifted but the city is in dire straits. Your subjects need immediate shipments of food and medicine, and look to their ever-benevolent Father and Augustus to care for them in the aftermath of their terrible losses.

Please listen closely to the delegation from Rome. They can tell you firsthand of the devastation. The people of Rome have paid the ransom for their city. Now they need your help.

Alaric asks for a lasting peace. His terms are reasonable, Brother. To secure our well-being, put aside your animus and negotiate with him. Peace at home, so you can deal with that usurper in Gaul, is in all our best interests. Let the Roman delegation and the Holy Father inform and guide your decisions. Please heed carefully their words. For the love of God and the Empire, give their advice great thought.

With sincerest wishes for your health and daily prayers for your long reign, your loving sister, by her own hand,

Galla Placidia Noblissima
Imperial Palace
Rome

"Good fortune to you, Attalus," she whispered as she folded and sealed the plea. "I've done all I can for the empire. Now it's time to restore my city—with or without my brother's help."

Chapter 17

Imperial Palace, Ravenna, January 409

Attalus suppressed a wince as Honorius glared at him and the Roman delegation. The emperor was not happy with the terms King Alaric dictated.

"I refuse to give the title of *magister militum* to anyone of that race!" Honorius fumed. His face reddened. Sweat anointed his brow as he brooded on his dais, back slumped, eyes darting around the room.

"Of course, Your Gracious Highness. That was merely a request by the Gothic king." Attalus bowed low. "It is your grace and power to give and take as you see fit." He stepped back into the delegation. *The princess was right about the emperor's temper. Now I understand why she fled the court!* Placidia had warned Attalus that, when Honorius became angry or obstinate, it was no use trying to persuade him. "Better to retreat and fight another day," she had advised. "It's best to flatter him, whisper in his ear, or bribe Olympius; but don't directly confront or contradict my brother."

"Your Most Noble Majesty." Pope Innocent stepped forward with a brief bow. "Take counsel from these older men, wise in the ways of this matter. Alaric's demands are quite reasonable, for what he will return."

Attalus looked in alarm at the Pope. *How would Honorius take this demand? Our good bishop hasn't learned much in his months at court.*

"I have had the counsel of old and wise men, and look where it's brought my empire. Britain, Gaul, and Spain are breaking away. A barbarian styles himself a king and makes demands of me. Soon, I will be emperor of nothing!" He scowled at Olympius, cowering by a sideboard.

It looks like the mighty Master of Offices is about to fall. That will be good news for Placidia. Who will next be in charge of our errant emperor? Attalus looked around the elegant receiving hall. Even the cedar burning in the winter braziers couldn't mask the reek of fear in the room. Only General Constantius, standing straight alongside the emperor's raised and gilded chair, seemed unfazed by the emperor's anger. The rest of the courtiers looked as if in danger of losing their heads. *Perhaps they are! No wonder the emperor is so ineffective. He needs a strong hand at his back.*

"But, Most Gracious Augustus, you can only gain—" Innocent tried to press his case.

"Enough!" Honorius rounded on the Holy Father, rage in his eyes, spittle flying from his lips. "More barbarians are pouring in from the north. My 'wise counsel' has failed to stop Alaric's brother-in-law and his cavalry from joining the Goths already infesting my lands. I will not be dictated to by that upstart Alaric, or by you. All of you! Get out of my sight!"

"Of course, Augustus," Attalus murmured with the rest of the courtiers as he hastily removed himself from the room. He slipped Placidia's letter in a fold of his immaculate, purple edged toga. *Better to deliver this later, when the emperor is in a calmer mood.*

"Prefect Attalus?"

He turned to confront a man in imperial livery. "Yes?"

The servant bowed. "General Constantius asks the favor of your company at tonight's evening meal."

"With the emperor?"

"No. At the general's private residence. He will send an attendant to lead you the way."

"Tell the general I will be happy to dine with him."

The servant bowed again and retreated to the receiving room.

Now that's an interesting development! What could the good general want with me?

ATTALUS ENJOYED HIS EVENING. Unobtrusive servants provided a rich meal and unwatered wine, while a beautiful young woman played her seven-stringed kithara in the background. The two men verbally jousted through a wide-ranging conversation about the situation in Rome and the rest of the empire. By the end of the meal, they were reclining comfortably on couches, with mutual accord. Attalus felt some kinship with Constantius; they both walked narrow paths through the shifting sands of troubled times.

"I believe Olympius will soon lose his place in the emperor's affections," Attalus said, sipping his wine. "His inability to contain the British usurper, and his failure to block the barbarian reinforcements, will be his downfall. Who do you think will fill his place?"

"Shrewd observation, Prefect." Constantius raised his eyebrows. "I've recommended Jovius, the former Prefect of Illyricum."

"That is good news for Rome! Jovius has treated with Alaric before. Perhaps he will be able to settle this matter. Our esteemed emperor would be wise to moderate his stance toward the barbarians and send them off to fight his enemies in Gaul."

"I agree. But I bear even better news: the young Eastern Emperor Theodosius is sending ten thousand elite Dalmatian troops to boost our depleted army. I hope to convince Honorius to send them to Rome in case negotiations with Alaric fail."

"That, indeed, is excellent news!" Attalus felt nearly giddy with relief. Or was it the warm wine and excellent food, after months of privation? He shook his head. It mattered not. He saluted his host with his wine goblet. "Thank you, General. In all ways, you've been a most excellent host."

Constantius hesitated. "Perhaps you might do me a favor of a...personal nature."

"How may I be of service?" *It would not be a bad thing to have this powerful man in my debt.*

"I understand you carry a message from Princess Placidia to her brother. How does she fare? Did she experience any hardship during the siege?"

"The princess is thinner—as are we all—but well. I made sure she received what stores could be spared. Her household did experience hardship. She lives with barely any servants."

"I'm distressed to hear that. She should have stayed in Ravenna, where she would have been safe." Constantius brooded for a moment. "Do you see her often?"

"As often as I can. She is very pleasant company."

"I see." Constantius scowled as he took a deep drink of his wine.

So that's how the wind blows! Attalus gave him a warm smile. "I don't think you do. The princess is a valued friend and ally, no more."

"I am glad to hear you are no rival for her affections, for I fear you would be a dangerous one. Does anyone else pay her court?" Constantius appeared to unconsciously hold his breath while waiting for an answer.

"Placidia, like good steel, has been honed and sharpened by the grinding necessity of adversity. She is growing from an innocent girl into a formidable woman—not one that an ordinary man would wish to take on."

"I'm not an ordinary man." Constantius snapped. "I value her intelligence and independence of spirit. That is what attracted me to her."

"Of course, General, but the Princess cannot bestow her favors where she wishes. That is the duty of her wise and loving brother. Do you have some aspirations on that front?"

"I have asked for her hand, but Honorius hesitates."

"Given the emperor's childless state, the man who marries Placidia might himself aspire to the purple, or, at the least, father the next emperor. Perhaps Honorius sees a bridegroom for his sister as a threat to his life. He seems to be a bit...cautious...about his person."

"As he should be, in these troubled times. I have served him loyally. I hope one day he will consent to my marriage to his sister." Constantius sighed. "The status of her birth is an impediment to my happiness, not a cause for rejoicing. If Placidia were a palace servant, I would have her for my wife."

"So speaks a man in love." Attalus chuckled. "If she were a servant, the status of her birth would be just as much an impediment to your affection."

"True," Constantius admitted with a crooked smile. "Will you stay her friend and look after her welfare for me?"

"I would do that without your asking. Do you wish me to carry any messages for you?"

Constantius removed a letter from the breast of his tunic. "I labored much over this. Written words are not my medium. Please convey this to the princess with my deepest personal affection."

"With pleasure." Attalus raised his goblet. "To a happy conclusion of all our concerns."

"THANK YOU, ATTALUS." Placidia received her brother's letter with a small frown.

"Any excuse to visit the lovely princess." Attalus bowed over her hand. "And I took the liberty of bringing a picnic basket and my finest wine. Some supplies are finding their way to the markets, but I'm afraid the prices are exorbitant and the selection poor."

"Wonderful!" Placidia, who knew Attalus to be a man who enjoyed his luxuries, looked forward to the meal and the company with only a small twinge of guilt. She scanned her brother's letter. It was long, rambling, and evidently taken down by a scribe while Honorius fumed.

"What news from your brother?" Attalus asked, not quite looking over her shoulder.

"None good." Placidia folded the missive. "I am to come before him in person if I wish to beg his forgiveness, and he harbors no love for Rome. He considers the senate to be fractious, obstinate, disloyal, and a general thorn in his side—although he chose a different body part for this sore affliction. I'm afraid he will be of no assistance."

"How very unfortunate. The senators will not take their dismissal lightly."

"Is there anything they can do about it?" Placidia shrugged.

His smile brightened. A glint shone in his eye. "At this moment, no. But eventually the emperor will need us again, and this city has a long memory." He picked up the basket and placed his hand against the small of her back. "Come! Let us repair to your triclinium and enjoy this wonderful repast upon which my cook worked so hard."

After a feast of wild ducks stuffed with chestnuts, leeks stewed with fish sauce, and a lovely confection of honey, nuts, and chopped apples, they relaxed on adjacent couches, sipping a sweet wine. Placidia sighed with pleasure. "It has been a long time since I've had the pleasure of such delicious food. Even now, most of the food is plain fare—bread and beans."

"I sent a special hunter out to obtain these." Attalus popped another ball of the confection into his mouth, chewing delicately. "Alaric left us little in the countryside. Cattle, pigs, fowl—all taken with the caravans. Cities to the south are sending supplies, but it takes time to herd cattle and pigs."

"The stolen animals will slow Alaric's progress as well. Where is he headed?"

"I last heard he was travelling to Tuscany to establish a winter camp. The army is over thirty thousand men, and he has another seventy thousand women, children, and slaves, plus heavily laden baggage wagons and the herds. He will move slowly."

"Is Olympius still in power in Ravenna?" Placidia contemplated her glass. "I see his hand in my brother's refusal to negotiate with Alaric. Caesar allied himself with the Celts to defeat the Germans. We should ally ourselves with the Goths to defeat the British usurper." The wine seemed to acquire a sour taste. She set it aside.

"I'm impressed with your military acumen, Princess, and appreciate your insight into the motives of those close to the emperor."

"I had a good teacher." Placidia sat silent a moment, looking at Attalus from beneath her lashes, a tingling sensation centered in her womb. He was a good-looking man of middle age, trim, only lightly marked by time. She was surprised by her body's reaction as she felt the heat crawling up her neck to her face. She ducked her head to take a sip of wine. *He is a charming man, and I am allowed the small pleasure of his company.*

Attalus had a lightness of spirit that appealed to her as a balance for her own seriousness. He was intelligent and clever, given to scholarship and sensual delights. He didn't lack for ambition but didn't seem to have the ruthless streak most successful men exhibited. Placidia believed he achieved his rank of Prefect because he was a candidate all could agree on—a likeable neutral figure and challenge to none.

Attalus certainly knows how to play the game of imperial courtier, but games aren't real. She sighed, resisting the attraction.

He reached across the couch to lightly touch her arm. "What troubles you, my dear?"

"Nothing." Placidia, embarrassed at being caught at her contemplation, covered up by asking, "Did you enjoy your stay at the court? Did you acquire any allies?"

"I met a number of influential men. One, in particular, asked after you."

"Who?" She frowned, wracking her brain for a possible candidate.

"Constantius."

"The General?" Placidia screwed up her face in a moue of distaste. "He's my brother's creature. Did you not find him a most peculiar man?"

"I found him an intelligent, amiable, and capable man. He provided me with a most impressive repast."

"Everyone knows the way to gain your affection is to provide a delicious meal. If Alaric himself provided you with choice meat and fine wine, you would declare him a most fine fellow," Placidia jibed.

"You wound me to the heart!" Attalus reclined in a fake swoon, hand over his 'wounded' chest.

Placidia laughed and said, to no one in particular, "With the prefect out of the way, there is more of this delightful confection for me." Whereupon Attalus bolted upright to vie for the last pieces.

With the spoils divided to both their satisfactions, Attalus continued on a more serious note. "Constantius is a powerful man, and an honorable one. He advises your brother well and takes no bribes. Two of our delegation tried to buy his favor. He banned them from the emperor's presence."

Placidia shuddered. "Something about the man repulses me."

"I am sorry to hear that, Princess." Attalus took a folded letter from his tunic. "He asked me to give this to you, with his deepest affection. You could do worse than ally yourself with such a man."

"I'll read this later." She put the letter aside and arched her brows at the prefect. "Would you not be disappointed if I looked favorably upon the General's suit?"

"I would not dare reach for the hand of a princess," Attalus said, as he did just that. He kissed her palm, sending waves of delight up her spine. "Please consider me a friend, in whatever capacity you find fitting and proper."

Placidia appreciated the playfulness but heard the note of truth in his words; he would not vie with Constantius for her hand. *It is just as well. I have no desire to entangle myself with a suitor—at this time.*

"Thank you, Attalus." She regretfully withdrew her hand. "You are one of my few friends, and I value your high regard. But it is getting late. I must not keep you from your duties."

He rose from his couch. "It is a sad duty that takes me from such charming company."

Placidia laughed. "I'll see you tomorrow, Prefect, to discuss equitable distribution of the supplies coming into the city. My charitable ladies want first choice to give to the poor, before the greedy merchants increase the prices beyond even our means."

"Tomorrow then, Princess."

PART III

THE USURPER

NOVEMBER 409 - AUGUST 410

CHAPTER 18

Rome, November 409

Damn the emperor for a pig-headed idiot!" Attalus muttered as he stalked through the agitated crowd in the forum, on his way to the Senate House.

His companion, an envoy from Alaric, leaned in to hear better. General Ataulf, an attractive man of middle height, dressed in a Roman cavalry officer's uniform, asked, "What?"

"Nothing!" Attalus shouted over the rumbling of the crowd. "The citizens of Rome are upset that your people have paid us a second visit."

He used to stroll through the city with only a servant in attendance. Now a dozen strong men protected him and the envoy from the frightened citizens. Most of the men in the forum were unarmed, but a few carried sticks or rocks that they brandished as they shouted: "The Goths are at the gates!" "What are we going to do?" "We have no army to protect us!"

Fickle Fortuna! I really thought the new Master of Offices Jovius could settle the Goth matter, but Honorius made a hash of it—again. Rebuffed, Alaric's army once more descended on Rome, taking up their old camps outside the northeast gates. Panic ruled the streets. People looted markets, hoarded food, retreated to their neighborhoods in armed gangs.

His party reached the steps, where a line of city guards kept the anxious people away from the senators, who were arriving in ones and twos. He pointed to the side of the brass doors. "Stay here until I call for you. You have to be invited in."

The general nodded and took his post next to the entrance, hand on sword.

Attalus left his escort to reinforce the guards, then stepped into the cool marble interior. He expected comparative peace but, while the senators did comport themselves with a sense of decorum, their conversations were tinged with panic. His stomach knotted in response.

The senators settled in their seats. Attalus took his place by the empty chair, calling the senate to order. Even the presence of barbarians at their gates could not negate the need for ceremony. Following the usual prayers and rituals, Attalus at last addressed the senate. "Fellow Senators, because our emperor has failed to establish peace, King Alaric of the Goths is at our gates for the second time in two years." There was grumbling at Attalus's blaming the emperor, but he couldn't discern whether it was agreement or outrage. He waited for the mutters to subside.

"We have choices to make as to how to meet this most recent threat. Before we do, we should know Alaric's position. He has sent an envoy to put his case before the senate. General Ataulf, please come before the Conscript Fathers."

The red-haired cavalry officer strode through the open bronze doors and down the center of the Senate House to Attalus' side. "This is General Ataulf, Alaric's brother-in-law and commander of his cavalry. He comes under truce and my protection. Please give him your attention." Attalus took his seat among the senators, who were stunned to silence.

The General looked around with calm attention, addressing the assemblage in flawless Roman. *He must have been schooled in rhetoric,* Attalus mused. Ataulf skillfully employed flowery praise for his leader, Alaric, and for the wisdom and glory of the senators, pitching his pleasant tenor voice to reach the back rows of the senate. Seeing the professional, dignified way Ataulf acquitted himself, it was difficult to assign the stereotype of a dirty, uneducated, bloody-minded barbarian to this man. Attalus looked around the room to see if others were impressed. He noticed several senators looking slack-jawed as their prejudices were severely tested.

After his flowery prologue, Ataulf launched into his appeal. "Senators. We are fellow citizens, yet our emperor treats us as invaders. Two generations ago, we fled from the Huns, who took our homelands in the east. Emperor Theodosius welcomed us, and is remembered among our people as a great friend. We served in your armies and led the assaults against your enemies. Multitudes of our comrades fell, to secure Theodosius Augustus sole reign over the empire. In return for our spilled blood, we asked only to settle our people in the empty hinterlands where we could farm and protect the borders."

A mutter rose from the anti-barbarian faction.

Ataulf waited for them to subside. "But the current emperor said 'No!' After all our faithful service, Honorius—son of The Friend of the Goths!—ordered our extinction. Our former Roman brothers-in-arms fell upon us, butchering us in the night. They murdered our wives and children!" The emotion in his voice testified to his grief.

The senators sat silent.

"After proving our might against Rome itself—" Angry buzzing from the senators interrupted him, briefly. "–King Alaric again went to Honorius, asking him to ratify the peace that you, Conscript Fathers, negotiated last year. Honorius again said 'No!' The emperor refuses to acknowledge the wisdom of the Senate of Rome. He refuses to give my people even the smallest province, compensation for protecting your borders, or the military honors due our great king!"

Ataulf took a deep breath, then raised his voice to shout, "Honorius is not fit to be ruler of this great empire! We demand the Senate overthrow him and acclaim another—one who will cherish all his subjects, acknowledge their worth, and lead us wisely in these dangerous times!"

Attalus sat stunned with the other senators. He had not expected Alaric to demand a new emperor. *Quite a bold move, for a barbarian prince!*

Confused shouts arose from the benches. Lampadius stood, cutting through the hubbub with his stentorian voice. "You want us to acclaim Alaric Augustus? That we will never do! No heretic barbarian will ever wear the diadem!"

A roar of agreement rolled around the room. Ataulf stood impassively, waiting for the general outrage to die down. Finally, he raised his hands. The sound subsided to an angry murmur.

"Our mighty leader has no designs on the diadem! He wants only to serve–" Silence reigned as his words took effect. "–as a military leader of this great realm. With Stilicho's untimely death, the Western parts of the empire are vulnerable to attack and civil war. The usurper from Britain even now heads south through Gaul to threaten Italy, and the Huns mass to the East, readying a vast army for invasion.

"You know how vulnerable you are." Ataulf paused to look around the room. "Let us protect you. Give us an emperor we can serve with honor and pride. Give us an emperor who has the wisdom to protect you and your fair city. Give us one of your own, and King Alaric will be yours to command!"

This time there arose a few shouts of agreement. Attalus was of two minds about the proposal. He did not condone overthrowing the rightful and consecrated emperor, but how would the city survive another siege? With nothing with which to pay off the Goths in booty, the people might be slaughtered or enslaved. Honorius had made his position clear. There would be no help from him. There must be another way...if the right person were declared emperor...one who was clever...who knew how to play both sides...

Ataulf's voice cut through his reverie.

"I leave you to your deliberations. King Alaric expects an answer no later than sundown tomorrow." Ataulf bowed to the assemblage and headed toward the bronze doors.

Attalus followed, clasping his hand once they were outside. "You will have your decision by tomorrow, General."

"I hope you make the right one," Ataulf said flatly, the threat obvious.

"My guards will escort you to the gate." He called over his captain, gave his orders, and returned to the Senate.

The debate that followed was heated and chaotic. Hard-liners argued against any dealings with Alaric, comparing his offer of protection to that of the street toughs who collected money from merchants as insurance against disrupting their business. Others protested on religious grounds, not wanting to give precedence to the heretical Arian Christians. Most pointed out that they could not stand against Alaric's army, they had no money to pay him off, and Emperor Honorius had, indeed, abandoned them.

In the end, the pragmatists carried the day. Several candidates for the new emperor were proposed and opposed by various factions. The senate only came together on one name. "Priscus Attalus, Prefect of Rome."

Attalus rose from his seat to loud exhortations. "My fellow senators!" he shouted. The men took their seats. "You do me too much honor. I argued in favor of a new emperor, but never sought the position for my self." *For good reason. I'll likely lose my head for this.* "I accept the acclamation, and will do my best for the people of Rome!"

The cries of his fellow senators filled him with pride. *This is the challenge of my life, but I can do this. I know how to play the game. I need to redirect the barbarians, protect the people, and survive as a usurper.* He looked around the room planning his strategy and counting his allies, then paused with a pang of regret. *Placidia. Will she accept me as emperor? For her own safety, I hope she doesn't. I'm sorry, Princess, to put you in this spot...again.*

PLACIDIA TWISTED AND UNTWISTED THE EDGE OF HER STOLA as she waited to see Attalus. He was to be officially acclaimed emperor on the morrow. She was grateful he had made time to see her before the ceremony. A servant showed her into his work room. Attalus dismissed his scribes and servants and offered her wine.

She refused with a wave of her hand. "Attalus, I consider you one of my dearest friends. You were kind to me when few were. You literally saved my life with good advice when Serena was arrested. I've come to return the favor. Do not do this thing. Your life is forfeit if you become a usurper."

"I know." He looked at her sadly. "But, like you, I have little choice. If we refuse King Alaric, the city will be under siege again. He will gain entry, slaughter the people, and put Rome to the torch. As emperor, I can save our city. I'll be in charge of Alaric's army. We can secure the African grain supply. This is our only option."

"But why you? Why not—" Placidia searched for a suitable sacrifice. "—Lampadius? He's a patrician and senior senator."

"Lampadius is too canny to take this role. From the bench he can thunder and fume with little or no risk. I've negotiated on Alaric's behalf, so he trusts me, and no one doubts my loyalty to this city. That makes me acceptable to both sides." He grinned at her. "All, that is, save you. Do you think I am not capable of being emperor?"

"You will certainly make a better one than my weak-willed brother."

He studied her face before replying, softly, "But not as good as your father?"

"It is not that." Placidia felt blood rush to her cheeks. "I am a princess. I cannot advocate the overthrow of the rightful emperor. My brother, with all his faults, is the son of the Great Theodosius and the rightful heir; acclaimed by the senate, the army, and the people of Rome; anointed by God to rule."

"The senate has acclaimed another, the army is in disarray, the people of Rome are in despair, and a bishop will anoint me in God's name."

"But you're a pagan!"

He shrugged. "I'm likely sacrificing my life for this. I can survive a sprinkle of water to become a Christian and save this city."

Her voice took on a pleading tone. "I came to you as a friend, but I too have an interest. My brother is childless and, given his…affliction…is likely to remain that way. Any son of mine will likely be his heir. With your ascension, I lose my imperial rank and the future of my children."

He took her hand and held it gently between his own. "If the British usurper is victorious, it's not just your rank, but your life, which is in peril. He already executed all your distant relatives in Spain. He is determined to wipe out the Theodosian line. With Alaric's army, we can smash him. If I am successful, your brother no longer controls your fate. I will put that back into your own hands."

"And if you are not successful?" Placidia asked.

"I have had a good life." Attalus gave her a crooked smile. "I have lived the way I wished; served my city and my people." His eyes brightened. "I do not anticipate failure. Alaric seeks to use me, but I will use him."

"I am of two hearts on this matter." She shook her head. "I pray to God for your well-being, but I cannot pray for the success of your venture. I must be loyal to my family."

"I understand." He kissed her lightly on the top of her head, then held her at arm's length. "As with Serena, we must have a public rift, but do believe I work secretly on your behalf and that of all the people of Rome. Continue your good work among the people. Keep their love, but repudiate me. If the worst happens, your brother must have no hint of our friendship, and you must seek his protection. Stay well, Princess."

Placidia left, troubled. *Oh, my friend, you play a dangerous game and there is little I can do to help.*

CHAPTER 19

Amphitheater, Rome, May 410

Are you sure about this, Princess? My missing leg's itching like it wants to run away," Paulus warned Placidia. He and a pair of stout guards accompanied her everywhere since Attalus had been acclaimed emperor: charity missions, visits to Aunt Laeta, and the occasional public entertainment, like the theater they attended today. She sometimes thought the men would troop into her bath if she let them.

"The crowd will settle once the show starts." She scanned the venue. Attalus, flanked by his Gothic guards, sat in the first-row center reserved for the imperial family. Senators, magistrates, and other dignitaries occupied the first rows. Other attendees, in strict order of rank and precedence, occupied seats from that point up to the top of the amphitheater, where the poorest people sat.

"There." She pointed to an unoccupied first row spot. Being the 'other' emperor's sister during the past six months left her rank ambiguous, so Placidia chose seats of the first order but not adjacent to Attalus' entourage. She did not want to appear to give sanction, even by proximity, to his imperial claims.

The comic mimes came out first and, in the best Roman tradition, put on a bawdy show with an actor clearly impersonating the emperor having sex with anything that moved, including a goat. Attalus laughed at the show, but most in the crowd didn't. The man playing the emperor bowed to a mere scattering of applause, and left the stage with a stiff smile. Angry shouting broke out in the upper reaches.

Placidia craned her neck to look toward the back seats. "The crowd seems upset. Perhaps we should leave at the intermission." The feeling of danger crawled up her spine. Public entertainments such as the theater and chariot races were the only venues where ordinary people could confront their leaders. Roman citizens had a tradition of petitioning emperors here, but this felt different. The anger seemed tinged with desperation.

"We're hungry!"

"Where's the bread?"

"Food! We need food!"

Placidia shook her head. She and her charitable ladies had less and less food to pass out to the poor as the days passed. *Damn you, Heraclian. It wasn't bad enough you murdered my uncle, but now you starve my people.* Count Heraclian had proved again to be a loyal subject to her brother. He had destroyed the small barbarian force sent to Africa by Attalus and promptly cut off the grain supply to Rome. She turned her gaze to Attalus. *Do something, my friend, before the people riot.*

Attalus stood to face the crowd. The protestors quieted, briefly. He adjusted his extravagant purple cloak.

"Citizens of Rome!" his voice boomed. "I know your hardship. I lived through the first siege with you. My belly went empty as well."

Disbelieving jeers and shouts arose from the crowd.

"The failure of the African venture was a disappointment to us all. But I assure you, food is on its way from the south as I speak. We will send more troops to defeat Heraclian and restore our food supply!"

"Why not just put a price on human flesh?" a young man shouted, referring to the government practice of regulating food prices and the acts of cannibalism rumored to have taken place during the first siege.

More angry shouts drowned out Attalus' attempts to calm the crowd.

"We should go now, Mistress." Paulus looked nervously around the agitated throng.

"Agreed. I have no desire to brook an angry mob."

Small missiles started to reign down on the front seats. The theatergoers had come prepared with potsherds and pebbles. They would not likely kill, but when thrown with force they could seriously injure.

Attalus' Gothic guard immediately closed ranks around the emperor and escorted him out of the exit reserved for him. The rest of the dignitaries were not so lucky. They stampeded for the common exits, causing more injuries than the flung stones.

"Hold, Princess, until the exits clear!" Her guards screened her from the barrage. One grunted in pain when a pebble struck him in the cheek, leaving a bloody gash. Paulus held one of their seat pillows over her head.

The crowd laughed and jeered at the escaping aristocrats, evidently satisfied with making their point. Placidia felt the mood of the crowd change subtly from menacing mob to something less. Still dangerous if roused, but not murderous.

"Paulus, wait." Placidia surveyed the crowd as it settled down. "Let's sit. It feels safer now. I wouldn't want the people to see a Theodosian run like the others."

A beefy man, who looked unaffected by the food shortage, stood and shook his fist at Placidia and her escort, now sitting alone on the first bench. "Hey, you rich *cunnus*! We don't want your kind here!"

"Shut up, you *culus*!" a woman shouted at him. "Don't you know who that is? Princess Placidia! She gave me food during the siege."

"She nursed my child!"

"She comforted me when my wife died!"

"She gave me clothes!"

The shouting continued until the people broke into a chant, "Long live Princess Placidia!"

Placidia stood, her heart full, tears threatening to spill down her cheeks. The crowd quieted, waiting for her to speak.

"Thank you, good people of Rome. You are in my prayers every day. I and the other charitable ladies will not abandon you."

A cheer went up from the crowd.

"I came here to see the dancers. Who would like to join me in these prime seats?" She indicated the empty front rows, with welcoming hands.

The people in the crowd turned shy, not wishing to intrude on space they had never been allowed to share.

"Please!" Placidia laughed, almost giddy in the wake of receding fear. "I don't like to sit alone."

A matronly woman shouted, "Only if you take the emperor's seat! You deserve it more'n he." A chorus urged her, "Take the emperor's spot."

Placidia smiled as she turned to Paulus. "You heard the people. Let's move." Her guards gathered up her cushions. They moved onto the center front seats, to shouts and whistles. Her confidence rising, Placidia turned to the audience. "Now join me!"

First a trickle—mostly women—then a steady flow of people shifted to the front of the theater, jostling good-naturedly for seats close to Placidia. Spying the Master of Ceremonies peeking out of a door on the stage, she called out, "Good Sir, bring on the dancers!"

The crowd laughed, stamping their feet as the dancers took center stage.

Placidia settled back onto her cushions with mixed feelings. Sitting in the emperor's seat gave her a heady sense of power. *So, this is what it's like to have the love of the people!*

After a moment savoring her victory, however, she remembered at whose expense it came. *Oh, Attalus, what is to become of you?*

CHAPTER 20

On the plains outside Rimini, June 410

Attalus sat behind a camp table in his field tent, looking over the latest reports of defections. One by one, the cities that had originally welcomed his ascension now repented, begging Honorius for forgiveness. Given his encounter at the theater, and the continued shortage of food, Attalus felt the city of Rome wouldn't hold out much longer.

He slammed the reports on the desk, startling his scribe and attendant. *If only the boy emperor in Constantinople hadn't sent more troops! I had Honorius on the run. He was within days of recognizing me, abdicating, and accepting banishment to an island. Now it's all falling apart.*

"Augustus, a word?" General Ataulf stood in Attalus' tent door. "Alone."

"Of course, General." Attalus dismissed his servants. The guarded look on Ataulf's face sent his blood racing. *I thought I had more days before the end. Can I talk my way into keeping my head, and protect Placidia?* Alaric had wanted the princess taken and held as the emperor's "guest" for weeks. While they had Honorius on the run, Attalus put it off as unnecessary. *Once I am no longer emperor?*

Ataulf took a folding camp chair and sat in front of the table. "King Alaric is not happy."

Straight to the point! Attalus offered him a brief smile. "We've experienced some temporary setbacks, but—"

"Jovius and his staff left the camp last night, and are reportedly on the road to Ravenna."

"That cowardly sycophant!" Attalus sat back in his chair. *The Ravenna rats are leaving the ship. I thought Jovius, at least, would remain faithful. I hope Honorius hands him his own head!*

Attalus rose to pour a goblet of wine from a pitcher on a sideboard. "Want some?"

Ataulf shook his head.

A barbarian refusing wine—a doubly bad sign. Attalus sat, gulped his vinegary drink, and grimaced. "Smart man. It's a wretched vintage." He set the goblet aside and leaned forward. "Ataulf, we've worked well together these last few months. I hope I can count on your friendship. How long have I got?"

"Astute, as always, my friend. We plan to negotiate one more time. General Constantius has already made overtures. Alaric plans to strip you of your regalia tomorrow in a formal ceremony and send it as a gift to Honorius."

"Along with my head?"

"That depends." Ataulf shrugged. "It might serve us to let you hold onto your head until the conclusion of the negotiations. Or Alaric can send it first as a sign of good faith and take the Princess Placidia as a hostage to guarantee that Honorius keeps his end of the bargain."

Attalus wiped sweaty palms on his thighs. *This is my last chance to save myself and Placidia.* He pasted a smile on his face. "I've worked with General Constantius. He's a fair and reasonable man. Give me sanctuary after my dethroning tomorrow and I could be a useful advisor during negotiations. As for the princess? She's but a rebellious half-sister. Honorius has made no effort to have her return to his court during these past two years, knowing you could take her anytime. He has shown he puts little value on her life, and she would be of no leverage."

Ataulf's eyebrows shot up. He snorted in disbelief.

Attalus turned his palms up in supplication. "I, on the other hand, am a valuable hostage—the usurper who humiliated Honorius by offering him his life in exile, minus his thumb and first finger. That slight cannot be easily forgotten. Don't offer my head until the negotiations are concluded. And," he shrugged, "if the talks break down, you know where the princess lives."

A slow smile broke across Ataulf's face. "You make several good points, my wily friend. Come join me at dinner. We can talk over the details. I'm sure, between the two of us, we can persuade my brother-in-law to a less bloody end to our friendship."

"Excellent!"

"I'll send an escort later." Ataulf headed for the tent door.

Attalus rose and slapped the general's back as he left the tent, but his sweat chilled as the Goth guards turned to face the tent, blocking his own exit.

At least they kept their swords sheathed—for now. I can convince Alaric of my worth, but how do I get word to Placidia to flee?

CHAPTER 21

Imperial Palace, Rome, July 410

Placidia sniffed at the garlicky sauce on the plate of eels laid out for an informal meal with Aunt Laeta and Lady Tisamene. She ordered a servant, "Take this back. The eels are too highly spiced for Lady Tisamene. Bring boiled beef instead."

A satisfied look flitted across the servant's face. After the famine last year, no food was wasted in the palace. The staff would share the leftovers among themselves. Placidia briefly had an uncharitable thought. *Did Cook deliberately create a dish she knew would be unsuitable for my elderly guest, as a treat for the staff?* She mentally shrugged. *Everyone occasionally deserved a treat.*

"Lady Laeta and Lady Tisamene," Paulus announced at the door of the small triclinium, then retired.

Scents of lavender and mint from the herb garden wafted into the room on a summer breeze. Open shutters provided soft natural light. A perfect setting for a celebratory visit. Heraclian restored the grain supply to Rome. Farmers from miles around flooded the city with summer bounty: melons, fruit, delicate greens, fish from the ponds and rivers, chicken, and eggs. With fall harvests coming, there would soon be fresh meat from the replenished herds. Rome healed. Placidia wanted to relax, take pleasure in her contributions to that healing.

Placidia greeted both women with a hug. "Welcome, Aunts!" She ushered them to cushioned seats with inlaid side tables to hold food and drink.

Discreet servants plied them with well-watered Falerian wine and small plates of delicacies while they talked. Tisamene looked on the repast, nodding approvingly. Placidia suppressed a chuckle. Tisamene approved of very little.

After the servants whisked away their bowls, emptied of honeyed nuts, berries, and cream, Placidia sipped her sweet wine, sighing with pleasure. Although Alaric had stripped Attalus of the purple, her friend survived with the Goths. From all reports, the talks between Alaric and Honorius proceeded well. *Life is good, for the first time in a long time. Now if only...*

"Aunt Laeta, how fares Tia?" Her frail cousin had miraculously survived the winter and even improved this spring.

"Much better. The warm weather suits her. She takes short walks in the garden, and reads. If the times were not so troubled, I would take her south, to the beaches at Naples."

"She still refuses to meet with me?"

Tisamene leaned forward to put a withered hand on Placidia's knee. "Give her time, my dear. She understands in her head that you had to agree to the senate's warrant, but in her heart, she still blames you for her mother's death."

"I understand." Placidia sat back, staring at her cup of wine, her good mood shattered. "I haven't forgiven myself. Why should I expect Tia to forgive me?" She drained her cup and held it out to an obliging servant.

The two older women exchanged worried glances. Tisamene huffed, "You won't find forgiveness or forgetfulness at the bottom of a wine jug. I thought you had already learned that lesson!"

Placidia set her goblet aside. "I have, Aunt. I didn't mean to worry you. I've taken your admonitions to heart and try to do God's work for my people and my soul. It helps."

"Good!" Tisamene leaned back in her chair. "Then we—"

"Princess!" Paulus interrupted from the door. "You have an important messenger."

A dusty young man, with dark smudges under his eyes, entered the room and handed Placidia a packet. "Apologies, Most Gracious Princess. This is a most urgent message from my master Attalus."

At close quarters, her nose twitched at the combined odors of human and horse sweat. *He must be a post rider. They can make the trip in two days.*

"Does the message require a reply?"

"No, Princess."

She nodded. "Paulus, please see that our messenger is fed and bathed before he leaves. Do you need a bed for the night?"

He bowed. "I have other messages to deliver, as soon as possible. I should leave now."

"As you wish. If, later, you find yourself in need of shelter, come back."

"Thank you for your kind offer, Princess." He flashed her a tired grin and left.

Paulus lingered in the doorway before Placidia dismissed all the servants. He then stumped away on his crutch, giving her a disappointed look.

Laeta and Tisamene sat silent while she broke the wax seal and quickly read the letter. *Good God!* The blood drained from Placidia's face. Feeling slightly faint, she dropped the letter in her lap and turned to her guests. "Attalus says the talks are going well, but warns that Alaric wants to take me hostage as a guarantee of Honorius' good faith. He advises I flee Rome by ship and sail to Ravenna, because the barbarians have no navy."

"Does he have any notion when Alaric will strike?" Laeta asked.

"He feels I should leave now, but no later than the end of negotiations."

"We'll make inquiries, so your name won't come up in case Alaric has spies abroad." Laeta rose as if to leave.

"Wait!" Placidia grabbed her hand. "I don't want to go to Ravenna."

"I understand you don't want to return to your brother's court, child. You can go to Constantinople, or Alexandria, or Jerusalem. We can arrange for funds at whatever city you care to visit."

"No! I don't want to leave Rome. I have a life here, friends, family." Placidia squeezed Laeta's hand. "My people need me."

Tisamene scowled. "You will do your people no good if you're carried off in one of those filthy barbarian wagons!"

"Two years ago, I took your advice. I still regret it. As with Aunt Serena, this seems to make sense, but things are different now. I have the love of the Roman people. If I abandon them, will they forgive me? Tia hasn't. Make inquiries, if you will, but I won't decide in haste."

"Don't leave it too long, child, or the decision will be made for you." Laeta freed her hand. "Come, Mother. Let's give Placidia time to think."

*****

Rome, August 410

"NEWS, PRINCESS." Paulus wheezed after making a limping run the length of the palace. "The emperor's troops attacked Alaric during negotiations. The Goths are on the march to Rome."

"Heaven help us!" Placidia put down her quill and sat back in her chair. *Again! Three attacks in two years! Brother, what lack-wit advises you now?*

They both turned their heads as a dull roar rolled up the Palatine hill from the forum.

"The people must be getting the news. Send a guard to find out what is happening."

Placidia paced, unable to concentrate on her correspondence. By the time one of the men guarding the palace shuffled in with Paulus at his elbow, Placidia checked to see if she had worn a path in the Persian carpet.

"Report, man!" Paulus ordered.

"Your Most Gracious Ex—"

"Just tell me what is happening in the streets," Placidia ordered, trying to calm her own frantic heart.

"Yes, Princess." The guard stood at attention. "The post rider from Ravenna declared that the Goths are at war again and heading for Rome. They will be here within three weeks."

"I know that!" Placidia wanted to throttle the man. "What is the senate doing? How are the people responding?"

"The senate called a session. They are gathering now. The people pack the forum, waiting to hear from the senators."

"Your assessment?"

"They're scared, Princess. There is no looting—yet. The people wait for answers and direction."

"Good. There is still time to prepare." Placidia chewed on her lower lip, then looked up at the guard. "Gather five of your fellows, but change into plain livery. I want to go to the forum and see for myself what the Senators propose. Meet me at the north servant's gate in a quarter of an hour."

"Yes, Princess." He backed out of the room.

"Princess—"

Placidia raised a hand, cutting Paulus off. "You cannot come with me."

"I was going to suggest that you not go," Paulus huffed. "It's too dangerous."

"No more dangerous than crossing the swamps of Ravenna or traveling the bandit infested roads to Rome or almost starving to death," she snapped.

One look at his stricken face, and she softened her tone. "I'm sorry, my friend. I am no longer a child to be coddled and looked after. These last two years have changed me. I hope for the better."

The old soldier squared his shoulders, offering her a weary smile. "You would make your father proud, Princess."

She placed a comforting hand on his arm. "Thank you. Now, where do we keep my old traveling cloak?"

PLACIDIA AND HER BEEFY GUARDS infiltrated the packed crowd in the forum and took places close to the front. She settled in for a long wait, figuring the toothless wolves of the senate would bluster and dither. Surprisingly, the senate adjourned after a brief session. Lampadius came to the Rostrum, the hallowed spot that had seen speeches by great ancient orators such as Caesar and Cicero.

He didn't have to settle the crowd. They stood hushed and expectant.

"Good people of Rome!" His stentorian voice boomed over the crowd. "The Goths advance on Rome, but we are ready. Your senate has strengthened the walls and increased the capacity of the warehouses. We have trained the vigiles and recruited more guards."

Angry shouts echoed across the forum.

"We can't take another siege!"

"What's different?"

"Where's the emperor?"

Lampadius shouted for order. "We can withstand another siege. We'll strip the countryside of food before Alaric arrives. He must feed women and children besides his troops. He will starve well before we do, but he won't stay. Our good father, Emperor Honorius—may God bless his name—has promised troops to drive him off."

What? Placidia snorted. *When did my brother grow a spine? I'll believe that when I see the soldiers with my own eyes.*

Lampadius continued, "Stay calm, good people, and listen to your city advisors. We will weather this storm and come out stronger than ever. Put your faith in God and the emperor. We are Roman! Show those weak barbarians what that means!"

The crowd roared its approval. They began to disperse as Lampadius left the Rostrum.

Placidia gave the senator credit for calming a situation that could easily have spiraled out of control and led to looting and rioting, but she didn't believe in the rosy story he spun. *What game are you playing, Lampadius?*

CHAPTER 22

Rome, early August 410

W*hat a difference two years make.* Placidia watched from the walls of Rome as people, mules, and carts streamed from the city. Rich patricians, merchants, even prominent churchmen fled. Those that remained turned to Placidia and her charitable ladies—although that cohort thinned over the past two weeks as husbands and fathers deserted the city, taking their women with them. *Two years ago, everyone tried to get into the city ahead of the Goths. Now they all flee. Then, I was a naïve child running to the shelter of Serena's arms. Now...*

She pulled her gaze away, turning to the captain of the city guards. "Where have you deployed your men?" Attalus had spent time and money shoring up weak spots during his tenure as emperor. With the defections and full warehouses, they probably had enough food to withstand several weeks of siege, but the walls had to hold.

"We're stationed at the gates, and at regular intervals along the walls," the graying captain informed her. "But we don't have enough men to patrol the streets or guard the warehouses against looting."

She nodded. "I'll see what I can do with the neighborhood watches and vagiles. I'll ask for volunteer youths and army veterans to be lookouts on the wall, which should also free up some of your men."

"Thank you, Princess." The captain gave her a relieved smile.

"I'll leave you to your duties, Captain. I have to inspect the warehouses, and then the hospitals."

Hours later, Placidia and her guard left the warehouses bursting with sacks of grain and amphorae of oil and wine. Some of the supplies were probably from her own southern lands. It gave her a warm feeling to think her farms helped feed the Roman people in this crisis.

Her guard pulled closer as they approached a crowded intersection. "What's the problem, Captain?"

"There seems to be a broken-down wagon blocking the street, Princess. People have to go around it in ones and twos."

Placidia looked at the lowering sun. She was already late to meet her aunts at the charity hospital. "When we get closer, offer to help move the wagon to clear the street."

As they approached, Placidia heard a familiar voice cursing the wagon master and his team of mules. Lampadius shouted at the beleaguered driver. "Are you as stupid as your animals? Didn't you check your wheels before you loaded?" The wagon, heavy with chests and household furniture, listed over the back right broken wheel. A large cohort of private guards attested to the value of the goods.

"Y-yes, Sir! All was well, but this is a much heavier load than I calculated."

"This is a mess! I'll have your hide, and your mules' too. You won't see a single coin for this!"

"Captain, bring the senator to me." Placidia pulled her company to the side.

Lampadius' ruddy face paled when he came into Placidia's presence. "Princess! Why are you out in the streets? This is a dangerous time to—"

"I don't need a lecture from you, Senator. I'm about the people's business. A better question is, why are you in the street, transporting chests filled with, what? Gold coins? Silver plate? Where are you taking your treasure?"

He moved closer. Placidia's guards conspicuously put their hands on their swords. Lampadius looked at them with disgust. "I have no intention of harming the princess. I only wanted to keep our voices from rousing the mob." He lowered his tone to a near whisper. "I am leaving this cursed city. My wife and children left early this week for Brundisium. I'm following them."

That's why I haven't seen your wife for the past week. I should have known something was wrong, Placidia thought. "You're abandoning the people of Rome

122

and running off to safety, after that rousing speech last week?"

"This city is doomed, and you know it," Lampadius hissed. "I said what I did to keep the peace. There would have been rioting and looting otherwise."

"And you would have lost your fortune earlier rather than later." Placidia looked him up and down with a sneer. "You're despicable. There are no troops coming from my brother, are there? That was a lie!"

Lampadius had the grace to blush at that. "Alaric's blood is up. He will put the city to the torch. I'm going, whether you like it or not. I'd advise you to leave as well, Princess, and take anyone you love with you. Sacked cities are charnel houses." Lampadius stomped back to the broken wagon.

I should have him arrested, the cowardly dog…if I could only think of a legal reason. Placidia shook her head. *I can't keep a free citizen from leaving the city.*

"Should we help the senator move his wagon, Princess?" her captain asked.

"No. He can shift for himself, since he has no care for others." She looked around at the thickening crowd. "Let's go back and cross farther north."

"As you say, Princess."

At last they made it to her final destination of the day: the charity hospital, run by holy women and supported by the imperial family. Placidia entered a side door of the large brick building that stood beside a dilapidated church in the slums of Subura. Neat rows of pallets covered the floor, with only three occupants. The holy women inventoried their medicines and supplies in a small storage area. Placidia waved them back to work when they stopped to bow. She went to the office, where she found Laeta and Tisamene poring over lists. They looked up from a battered desk as she entered.

"Aunts!" Placidia stepped around the desk to hug Laeta, and kiss Tisamene on the cheek.

The lines on their faces seemed deeper, their eyes wearier, even as they greeted her with warmth.

"We were worried, child. You're so late." Laeta indicated a chair. "Sit. You must be exhausted from the day."

"I am." She dropped into the chair, energy draining from her. "I'm sorry I'm so late. The streets were clogged with people leaving. We ran across Lampadius decamping for Brundisium."

"Lampadius?" Laeta shook her head.

"Good riddance! Let the cowards run. That's fewer useless mouths to feed," Tisamene scoffed.

"He told me Honorius is not sending troops. Lampadius lied to reassure the crowd and ensure he could leave with a minimum of fuss. He advised me to flee, and take all whom I love with me."

The two women glanced at each other.

"What?" Placidia asked.

Laeta cleared her throat. "I believe you should go."

Placidia glared at her. "I thought we settled that two weeks ago. You want me to run away now? Abandon my people?"

"No, child—"

"I'm not a child, Aunt Laeta!"

"No, Placidia, you are not a child." Laeta looked sorrowful. "You are sister to the emperor, and will be held hostage if Alaric takes the city, possibly even killed. At the very least, the Gothic King will use you against your brother. Attalus kept you safe while he ruled, but that is no longer the case. I believe you should leave Rome, take yourself off the game board. I've arranged for a ship at Portus to take you by sea to Ravenna. It leaves tomorrow on the morning tide."

"And you, Lady Tisamene? Do you agree?" Placidia turned to the older woman.

A look of pain flashed over Tisamene's face. "My daughter speaks alone on this. She is right that you have a duty to your brother. You also have a duty to the people of Rome. You have led them well. I leave it to you to decide which is most compelling. I will not judge you for either choice."

"I see." Placidia sat, chewing her lip. When there was the slimmest possibility that her brother's troops were on the way to Rome, she had no problem making the decision to stay. Now? Her life might be forfeit. She had made the decision once before to save her own life, at the expense of her Aunt Serena, and regretted it.

"Take the rest of the day to think on it, but no more. Alaric draws closer. You have little time," Laeta pleaded.

Placidia's gaze turned inward. She remembered all the faces she had encountered that day: men, women, children taking hope and comfort from her presence; guards, bureaucrats, and city elders listening to her advice, taking her commands. She returned her attention to her Aunt Laeta and Lady Tisamene. "I don't need the time. I know where my duty lies. It is here, in Rome. I've been all over the city today. The walls are sound, the warehouses are full of food, the hospitals are ready. *I am ready, for whatever comes.*" Placidia's voice quavered with unshed tears as she appealed to the two women who had become closer to her than any other. "I hope you take some pride in me."

Laeta took her in her arms. "We do, Placidia. More than you could ever know."

"Enough talking," Tisamene croaked. "We have work to do."

"Yes, Lady Tisamene." Placidia smiled at the old woman. "We do."

*****

Placidia continues her adventurous life of power and intrigue in
Twilight Empress: A Novel of Imperial Rome.
(Theodosian Women Book #1)

Don't miss this "addictive read" (*Kirkus Reviews*); "filled with romance, political intrigue, and drama that will keep you turning the pages." (*History from a Woman's Perspective*)

Scan the QR code to buy *Twilight Empress* direct from the publisher. Available in print, eBook, and audiobook wherever books are sold, or inquire at your local library.

AUTHOR'S NOTE

Becoming the Twilight Empress almost didn't happen. Here's the story: I fell in love with the Theodosian women many years ago when I was writing my first book, *Selene of Alexandria,* which featured a fictional student of the historical Hypatia, Lady Philosopher of Alexandria. As I researched the life and times of Hypatia, I kept running across these great women: Placidia, who ruled the failing Roman Empire in the West, Pulcheria, who set the stage for the rise of the Byzantine Empire in the East, and Athenais, a poor pagan scholar who captured the heart of a Most Christian Emperor.

They each had compelling human stories that I wanted to share with my readers. Consequently, *Twilight Empress,* covering Placidia's life from the final Gothic siege of Rome until her death, came out in 2017. *Dawn Empress,* covering Pulcheria's life, came out in 2020 and Athenais' story *Rebel Empress* will be out in 2024. In editing *Twilight Empress,* I decided to shorten the book, and chopped off the initial chapters. Starting Placidia's story with her abduction by the Goths felt right. (Not a spoiler; this happens in the first pages of the novel.) Those early draft chapters covering her escape from Ravenna and hardships during the first two sieges languished in old computer files.

However, those abandoned pages nagged at me. I always wanted to cover that harrowing time when the Goths besieged Rome three times in two years. I felt those challenges shaped Placidia into the formidable young woman she was at the beginning of *Twilight Empress.* The escape from Ravenna is totally surmised. Most historians feel she resided in Rome, but we don't know for sure. However, she had her reasons for avoiding her brother's court and not returning when she had the chance to leave before any of the Goth sieges. In the absence of facts, it's the novelist's gift to fill in the story with their own fiction. I decided it made a better story to delay her leaving for Rome until after the execution of Stilicho, so she could accompany her ill cousin, the repudiated Empress Thermantia.

In addition, writing *Becoming the Twilight Empress* allowed me to deal with a piece of history that always bothered me. Why would Placidia give her consent to the senate to have her cousin/foster-mother Serena executed for treason during the panic and confusion of the first siege of Rome? The primary sources state that action as a fact. The secondary ones give various theories on how involved Placidia had been in the act: from reluctant verbal consent to a delegation of the Senate (depicted in my story) to her actively petitioning the senate in person and denouncing her foster-mother.

Stewart Irvin Oost in *Galla Placidia Augusta: A Biographical Essay* says of this black deed: "It is possible that Placidia did in fact sincerely believe in the treason both of Stilicho and Serena and was confident that she was acting in an emergency in the best interest of the state. But it is hard to believe that she was convinced the woman who had brought her up was in fact in collusion with Alaric against Rome. *The only explanation* (emphasis mine) must be that Placidia was already so prejudiced against Serena, disliked her so cordially that she could entertain the notion of the reality of her guilt on this occasion and concur in the decree condemning her to death."

Oost believes this is the more charitable interpretation, rejecting the theory that Placidia cold-bloodedly seized the occasion to kill Serena because, "we find no other incident in the admittedly scanty information about her life that would substantiate such a hypothesis about her character and Placidia, at least in later life, was a devout Christian." Other modern historians disagreed and felt Placidia was that bloody-minded.

I think Oost and his fellow historians were too narrow in their thinking. As Oost states, we have scanty information—no diaries, letters, or contemporaneous reports to give us insight into the motivations behind the act. Placidia *could* have hated her foster-mother and wished her dead—it was a violent time and imperial families were not immune to assassinating one another. She *could* have sincerely believed Serena was colluding with the enemy and her execution was an act of public safety. She also could have been so fearful for her own life, given the mood of the city after her brother refused to help Rome, that she would do anything to divert attention away from herself during the threatened riots and onto another imperial scape-goat—a theory not proposed by the historians.

As an author, I chose to present a motivation I thought just as valid as any of the above. Placidia could have reluctantly gone along with the Senate because the woman who raised her asked her to save herself. Serena was a skilled politician who had successfully maneuvered the imperial courts for two generations. She was acknowledged as the only one who could sooth her uncle Theodosius' violent tempers and she raised her younger cousins Honorius and Placidia after his death. At this time in Rome, her husband and son had been executed for treason, her daughters were dead or dying. Serena could have known her time had come. She didn't want to take Placidia down with her and the vulnerable young princess reluctantly went along with it.

It's as good as any other theory and fits my story better. I wanted to show how Placidia became the tough, capable woman we meet at the beginning of *Twilight Empress*. Serena could have been a significant role model. Since she died relatively early in the story, I used two other imperial women to help Placidia on her journey: her Aunt Laeta and Laeta's mother Lady Tisamene. They both resided in Rome at the time and ancient historians give them credit for assisting the poor during this time of crisis. Also, I needed someone to care for Thermantia, the rejected empress, whom I was surprised to find out survived all the chaos and "died in obscurity" in 415.

There's no direct evidence Laeta and Tisamene had any relationship with Serena, Thermantia, or Placidia. But, given they were all imperial ladies in the same city, it stretches the imagination to think they had no communication or awareness of each other's plights. I like to believe that, in her time of loss and confusion, Placidia had the love and guidance of these experienced older female relatives, ones who could help her accept loss and move onto the path of duty she would assume. Placidia came out of these years stronger, and much less naïve, to take her place in the imperial pantheon of formidable Theodosian Women.

I would love to hear from you about your reactions to the story and characters. You can contact me at my website (faithljustice.com) or leave a comment on my blog.

Finally, I need to ask a favor. I'd love a review of *Becoming the Twilight Empress*. Loved it, hated it—please give me your feedback at your favorite book review sharing site. No need for a literary critique—just a couple of sentences on what you liked/didn't like and why. Reviews can be tough to come by these days, and having them (or not) can make or break a book. So, I hope you share your opinion with others. If you review on Amazon, scan the QR code below to be taken directly to the review page.

Thank you for reading *Becoming the Twilight Empress.*

Faith L. Justice
Brooklyn, NY

Scan for Amazon review page:

Glossary

agentes in rebus—imperial spy and messenger network controlled by the Master of Offices.

Arian heresy—a nontrinitarian Christian sect that believed Jesus Christ to be the Son of God, created by God the Father, distinct from the Father and therefore subordinate to the Father. Named after Arius (c. AD 250–336), a Christian presbyter in Alexandria, Egypt. Many of the barbarian tribes were converted to Christianity by Arian missionaries under the Arian Emperors Constantius II (337–361) and Valens (364–378). The Council of Nicaea of 325 declared Arius a heretic, but he was exonerated, then again denounced at the Ecumenical First Council of Constantinople of 381.

culus—Latin word for anus, equivalent to today's epithet "ass-hole" (not considered as offensive as *mentula* or *cunnus*).

cunnus—vulgar Latin word for female vulva, equivalent to today's epithet "cunt."

diadem—"band" or "fillet;" originally in Greece, an embroidered white silk ribbon, ending in a knot and two fringed strips often draped over the shoulders, which surrounded the head of the king to denote his authority. Later made of precious metals and decorated with gems. Evolved into the modern crown.

fibula (singular) *fibulae* (plural)—an ornamental clasp designed to hold clothing together; usually made of silver or gold but sometimes bronze or other material; used by Greeks, Romans, and Celts.

forum (singular), **fora** (plural)—a rectangular plaza surrounded by important government buildings at the center of the city; the site of triumphal processions and elections; the venue for public speeches, criminal trials, and gladiatorial matches; the nucleus of commercial affairs.

Gaul—a region of Western Europe inhabited by Celtic tribes, encompassing present day France, Luxembourg, Belgium, most of Switzerland, parts of Northern Italy, as well as the parts of the Netherlands and Germany on the west bank of the Rhine. Rome divided it into three parts: Gallia Celtica, Belgica and Aquitania.

Goths—an early Germanic people, possibly originating in southern Sweden; they are mentioned by Roman authors as living in northern Poland in the first century AD; during later centuries they expanded towards the Black Sea, where they replaced the Sarmatians as the dominant power on the Pontic Steppe and launched a series of expeditions against the Roman Empire.

Huns—a nomadic group of people who lived in Eastern Europe, the Caucasus, and Central Asia between the first century and the seventh century AD; may have stimulated the Great Migration, a contributing factor in the collapse of the Western Roman Empire. They formed a unified empire under Attila the Hun, who died in 453; their empire broke up the next year.

kithara—seven-stringed instrument of the lyre family.

kohl—black eyeliner originally used by Egyptians and others in the East to protect the eyes from bright sunshine, later as a cosmetic.

magister militum—"Master of the Soldiers;" a top-level military command used in the late Roman Empire, referring to a senior military officer equivalent to a modern war theatre commander.

magister utriusque militia—"Master of both branches of the soldiery;" the highest rank a general can achieve.

mentula (singular)/*mentulae* (plural)—vulgar Latin word for penis, equivalent to modern epithet "dick" or "prick"

nobilissima puella, nobilissimus puer—"Most Noble Girl/Boy;" title conferred on imperial children by a sitting Augustus before given a higher title.

palla—outermost rectangular woman's mantle/shawl worn over the shoulders and hair; could be as complicated as a toga or as slight as a scarf.

paludamentum—originally a cloak or cape fastened at one shoulder, worn by military commanders. After Augustus, only emperors wore them. As supreme commanders of the Roman army, they were often portrayed wearing it in their statues and on their coinage.

Portus—Rome's primary seaport, built by Emperor Claudius to handle large merchant ships including the grain fleet.

prefect—the chief minister of territories (city, province, etc.) equivalent to mayors in cities and governors in provinces.

scholae—an elite troop of soldiers in the Roman army created by Emperor Constantine the Great to provide personal protection of the emperor and his immediate family.

solidus (singular) ***solidi*** (plural)—a gold coin introduced by Emperor Diocletian in 301 as a replacement for the aureus; entered widespread circulation under Constantine I after 312.

stoa—a classical portico or roofed colonnade.

stola—long, pleated dress, worn over a tunic, generally sleeveless, fastened by clasps at the shoulder called *fibulae*, usually made of fabrics like silk, linen, or wool, worn as a symbol representing a Roman woman's marital status.

Subura—the poorest neighborhood in Rome consisting of tall apartment buildings and situated over a drained swamp between the Roman hills.

Suevi—a large group of related peoples who occupied more than half of Germania and were divided into several distinct tribes under distinct names. At one time, classical ethnography had applied the name "Suevi" to so many Germanic tribes that it appeared as though in the first centuries

A.D. this native name would replace the foreign name "Germans." In 259/60, a group appears to have been the main element in the formation of a new tribal alliance known as the Alamanni east of the Rhine and south of the Main; they later joined the Vandals and Alans invading Gaul and Spain.

tisane—herbal teas; beverages made from the infusion or decoction of herbs, spices, or other plant material in hot water.

triclinium—a formal dining room in a Roman building used for entertaining guests; could hold multiple couches arranged in a hollow "U" shape; each couch was wide enough to accommodate three diners who reclined on their left side on cushions while household slaves served, and others entertained guests with music, song, or dance.

tunica interior—woman's tunic (usually with sleeves) worn under a *stola*, frequently longer, so the layers of fabric showed.

vigiles—or *vigiles urbani* ("watchmen of the city") were the firefighters and police of Rome.

ACKNOWLEDGMENTS

It has been my pleasure to write this story and bring these characters and this time to life. Among the many people who helped and encouraged me, I want to particularly thank the members of my writers' group *Circles in the Hair*. For more than thirty years, they have been there for me; reading drafts of my stories and novels, providing insightful feedback, and encouraging my dreams. They read several drafts of this book. Additional thanks go to my beta readers who provided invaluable feedback: Eileen Donovan, Laura Eppich, Kate Hornstein, Allison Macias, and Susan Wands. Special and loving thanks go to my husband Gordon Rothman for supporting me in countless ways; and to my daughter Hannah, who grew up sharing me with my writing career and showing no sibling rivalry whatsoever.

No historical fiction acknowledgment would be complete without thanks to the librarians who tirelessly answer questions and find obscure documents. My special thanks go to the New York Public Library—a world class institution. I consulted dozens of books there and hundreds of articles but relied most heavily on the research of Stewart Irvin Oost in his *Galla Placidia Augusta: A Biographical Essay* and Kenneth G. Holum in his *Theodosian Empresses: Women and Imperial Dominion in Late Antiquity*. A bibliography of the most useful works can be downloaded from my website (faithljustice.com).

Although I tried to get it right, no one is perfect. If the reader should find any errors of fact in the book, please know they are my own and not those of my sources. Please get in contact at my website (faithljustice.com) and let me know, so I can change subsequent editions.

Again, thanks to all who helped make this book possible with special thanks to those of you who read it and share it.

ABOUT THE AUTHOR

FAITH L. JUSTICE writes award-winning fiction and articles in Brooklyn, New York. Her work appears in such publications as *Salon.com, Writer's Digest,* and *The Copperfield Review.* She was Chair of the New York City Chapter of the Historical Novel Society for five years and is still active on their Steering Committee. She is currently an Associate Editor for *Space and Time Magazine.* She co-founded a writers' workshop many more years ago than she cares to admit to. For fun, Faith likes to dig in the dirt—her garden and various archaeological sites. Sample her work, check out her blog, or ask her a question. She loves to hear from readers.

Connect with Faith online:

LinkedIn: https://www.linkedin.com/in/faith-l-justice-53974719/
X (formerly Twitter @faithljustice): https://twitter.com/faithljustice
Facebook: https://www.facebook.com/faithljusticeauthor/
Instagram: https://www.instagram.com/fljusticeauthor/

Scan the QR code for Faith's website/blog
https://faithljustice.com

RAGGEDY MOON BOOKS

raggedymoonbooks.com

www.ingramcontent.com/pod-product-compliance
Lightning Source LLC
Chambersburg PA
CBHW071925130726
47909CB00014B/2589

* 9 780917 053306 *